Where the
Great Hawk Flies

Where the
Great Hawk Flies

LIZA KETCHUM

Clarion Books
New York

Clarion Books
a Houghton Mifflin Company imprint
215 Park Avenue South, New York, NY 10003
Copyright © 2005 by Liza Ketchum

The text was set in 13-point Perpetua.

www.houghtonmifflinbooks.com

Printed in the U.S.A.

Library of Congress Cataloging-in-Publication Data

Ketchum, Liza, 1946–
Where the great hawk flies / by Liza Ketchum.
p. cm.
Summary: Years after a violent New England raid by the Redcoats and their Revolutionary War
Indian allies, two families, one that suffered during that raid and one with an Indian mother and
Patriot father, become neighbors and must deal with past trauma and prejudices before they can
help each other in the present. Based on the author's family history. Includes historical notes and
notes on the Pequot Indians.
ISBN 0-618-40085-0
[1. Prejudices—Fiction. 2. Vermont—History—18th century—Fiction.
3. Pequot Indians—Fiction. 4. Indians of North America—Connecticut—Fiction.
5. Conduct of life—Fiction.] I. Title.
PZ7.K488Whe 2005
[Fic]—dc22
2004029832

ISBN-13: 978-0-618-40085-0
ISBN-10: 0-618-40085-0

MP 10 9 8 7 6 5 4 3 2 1

For my sons,
Derek Ketchum Murrow and Ethan Ketchum Murrow,
and in memory of my great-uncle Carlton Griswold Ketchum,
who encouraged me to tell this story

Where the
Great Hawk Flies

Messenger

The hawk lifts
from the oak tree
catches an updraft
wheels above the raw stumps
of a new pasture,
crests the hilltop.

Wings beating,
her shadow glides over a mouse
trembling in the corn stubble.

The hawk plummets,
talons outstretched,
when a musket shot slices
the dawn silence.
Horses wheel and whinny
oxen bawl
a woman screams
and the mouse scampers
to safety.

The hawk rises
as flames devour houses barns animals haycocks.
She flies over dense timber
away from booming guns

galloping hooves,
the howling of men.

Below,
a shock of yellow hair bobs and dips
as a boy runs
through the underbrush,
arms pumping.

Although her nest
in the crook of a tree
is abandoned,
fledglings flown,
instinct drives her.
She dives,
sounding her warning:
"Kee-er! Kee-er!"

The boy raises an arm
shields his face,
disappears
beneath a rotten log.

The hawk beats into the wind.
Miles north,
driven by an empty belly
she spots movement
in a hemlock ravine.

Wingtips brush the feathered branches
as she glides
over a woman
who lugs one child on her back
while another clutches the dark braid
swinging at her waist.
The hawk dips a wing
and the woman follows,
scrambles beneath a tumble of boulders,
and pulls the children behind her.
They vanish.
Guns rumble in the distance.

The hawk keeps flying
circling

                                           and higher

                        higher

  higher

above the crack of muskets.
She catches a warm updraft
sails over the ridgeline
away from the furor of war,
and fades into the moist
tendrils of clouds.

Royalton Raid, October 16, 1780

Griswold, Vermont

October 1782

Part I

✷

A Visitor from the South

1. Daniel

First light.

I sat up, keeping quiet. My breath made smoke. Ice studded the iron roofing nails of our loft. Rhoda's face was ruddy atop her quilt.

We'd had a great frost.

Was I too late? I must hurry. I slipped off my pallet, pulled on drawers, breeches, wool shirt. Slid belly bump down the ladder and tiptoed to the front chamber, where a fresh fire crackled. No sound from behind the curtain where Mother and Father slept. Father would be in the barn already. He'd expect me to help him with the chores. But still—

'Twas my birthday, and the sun barely peeking over the hill. Surely I could skip the chores this once. It might be my last chance till spring.

Jody's tail thumped and I stilled her with my hand. "Good dog. You stay," I whispered. I wiggled into my jacket, lifted the latch, and went out.

The world was white and shining. Frost coated every

blade of grass, whitewashed the tips of corn tassels so they looked like the tails of *A'waumps,* the red fox. Sheep muttered in the barn and one of the oxen bellowed as I dashed past. Would Father see me? I stayed low, zigzagged through the cornstalks, and ducked into the woods under the hemlocks. Safe so far.

I crept to the stream bank, keeping to the shadows. A skim of ice floated over the deepest part of the pool, and the water rippled free only in the open. Would I find him?

Dead leaves clogged the branches of my fish weir. "If luck is with me, he'll show himself," I whispered. But what if he'd already gone to sleep for the winter?

I slid onto the flat rock and lay on my belly, waiting for the sun to reach the pool. First it stroked the high leaves of the maple with gold; then it warmed my moccasins, next my breeches. Finally, it touched my shoulders and lit the pool, making the ice sparkle—

There! Mr. Trout slipped from his hiding place under the roots of the maple. Long as my forearm, he swam slow and regal as a *real* king, not like that silly King George we trounced in the war. The spots on Mr. Trout's back flickered in the sunshine. I licked my lips, tasting him already. *You're mine.*

Mother would chide me, remind me to thank *Cautantowwit,* our creator, for bringing me this trout. Was *Cautantowwit* with me? *Thank you,* I told him, just to be sure, but fixed my eyes on Mr. Trout. Slow and careful, I rose onto my knees. Pushed up my sleeve. Lowered my hand—

Snap! A branch broke.

Ker-plash! A stone fell into the pool, soaked me from chin to belly. The trout slipped away. I jumped to my feet.

"Who's there?"

"Caught you!" A strange boy jeered at me. He hopped from foot to foot on the far bank, like someone dancing on hot coals.

"Fool!" I shook my fist at him. "What did you do that for?"

"'Cuz you're a dirty *Injun,* that's why. A savage." He spat at me, but his spittle turned on him in the wind.

I bit the inside of my cheek so he'd not see how his words stung me. What an ugly face! He was pale as corn samp, and his yellow hair stuck up in a cowlick on the back of his head. "We've a gander looks like you," I called. "For tuppence, I'll dust your back."

His mouth gave a sudden twist, his eyes opened wide, and he dashed away, his head tucked as if I might really throw him down—though I was on the far side of the brook. Was he that afraid of me? I laughed. "Buffle brain!" I jeered at him. "Yellow coward!"

He clapped his hands over his ears and disappeared under the hemlocks.

I leaned against the maple. My heart chattered loud as the squirrel complaining over my head. Who *was* that? I rubbed my jacket with my hands, as if that word he'd spat at me had stained the deerskin. *Injun.* A word no one spoke in our house.

He'd left two wooden buckets on the far bank. I crossed

on the log Father had set there last spring, and lifted a bail. The bucket was empty.

"He'll be thirsty—and come back." I set the bucket down and puzzled it out. The ugly gander boy was fetching water, for someone close by—but who, and where?

Only seventeen families in Griswold and no boys near my own age. The blacksmith complained of his four daughters. Mr. Shaw, who carried the freight to Boston, had only little Ephraim, smaller than my sister, Rhoda. Timothy Ellis, at the farm next to ours, was taller than Father now. And where was someone to live, here on our hill?

Then I knew. The abandoned cabin in the woods, once belonging to Mr. Amidon, where Father and I hunted for turkeys. The Amidon family left town two years hence, soon after the raid.

The raid. I didn't like to think on that terrible day, or what happened after. Father said it was past, and we should forget. But none of us could.

The Amidons had no children when they moved off, so it must be a different family. When Father and I were up to the cabin last spring, it was hardly fit for swine. "Swine." I laughed out loud. "About right for that gander boy."

I peered into the pool as I crossed the log, but Mr. Trout had gone back to sleep. I jogged for the house, my hands empty and cold.

Not even breakfast time, and my birthday already spoiled.

2. Hiram

Injuns, ready to dust my back. They might kill me!

I took off running, away from that boy and his yelling, but the noises chased after me, piling on so fast I covered my ears. Like it happened yesterday, I heard it all again: Gunshots, women screaming bloody murder, oxen bawling. I seen it, too: our house afire. Ma hiding in the privy while the Injun scooped me up, tossed me onto his horse like a sack a barley, the hatchet in his hand. Worst of all, our dead neighbor stared up at me, his eyes bugged out, face all twisted.

I fell down under a tree and squinched my eyes shut, but I couldn't chase away that fright. No matter the war was over, the raid long past, still the nightmare followed me day and night, sleeping or waking. It come on when I weren't even thinking on it. Eyes closed or open, I still saw Uncle Abner stumble around our foreyard, heard him bellow loud as his own ox. Saw the Injuns chase after him with spears, heard him howl for me as the Injun carted me away. Would I never forget?

"Hiram! Hi-i-ram!"

I uncupped my ears. Sat up and listened. Rubbed my eyes. I weren't on that Injun horse, but laying on the wet ground. And I weren't in Royalton. No, we was miles upriver, in some new place called Griswold. There weren't no house on fire, just red leaves in a maple tree. No screams—

just a sight of jays, scolding me. And in the distance, Pa. Calling me home.

"Hiram!" Pa hailed me again. I put my fingers in my mouth and whistled, the way Uncle Abner taught me afore the raid, afore the fire that ruint our farm and sent us running back to Connecticut like dogs with their tails tucked under their bellies.

I followed Pa's voice through the timber. What a fool I was. Skairt by a boy hardly bigger than me. Was he even there, or had I seen it all in my dream?

I jogged down the hill. It weren't until I reached the clearing that I remembered the buckets. I'd forgot to fill them, forgot to tote them home. Pa would lay the switch on me for sure.

But I was lucky this time. Pa and Ma was right where I'd left them, out in the foreyard having words. I ducked behind a big oak. Pa's back was to me and his shoulders was slumped.

"I told you we should stay in Connecticut," Ma said. "But no. You had to haul us back to Vermont, to a place more godforsaken than the one we lost two years ago." Her hands made fists acrost her apron and her face was fierce under her bonnet.

"Hannah. Please. What choice did we have?"

"Aren't you ashamed? Look at this. Grass so high in our chamber, it's food for our ox. Is that any way to live?"

I peeked out from behind the tree and followed Ma's pointing hand. Sure enough, through the open door I spied

Jed inside the house, his tail swishing while he ate up what should a been our new floor. And Ma was right. The cabin weren't much to look at: holes in the roof, the door hanging from one hinge, and gaps between the logs big enough for me to stick my fist through. No wonder she was mad.

Ma caught sight of me. "Hiram, come over here!"

"Yes ma'am." I dragged my feet.

"Go inside," Ma said. "Tell me. Is this a house, or a pigsty?"

"Looks like a barn for the ox," I told her.

Pa sighed. "It's all we've got." He pointed at the wagon. "Hiram, fetch some sacks."

Our wagon was piled with goods Pa hoped to sell when we opened our new store. I hoisted a heavy one, full of barley seed, and followed Ma inside. Pa clapped his hands and shooed Jed out into the clearing.

Ma started in wailing. "Look at this!" she cried.

I set down the sack and stared. A big old stump sat in the middle of the chamber, rooted in the ground like a tree could grow right through the holes in the roof.

"I guess it might work for a table, since we ain't got a real one," Pa said.

He meant it for a joke, but Ma plopped herself down on the stump, pulled her apron over her face, and bawled. Pa tugged his ear so hard, I thought he might tear it off.

"There's naught but bad luck in these hills," Ma cried. "It's sorrowful enough we lost our first house in the raid— now we have to live like animals! And you know I despise these dark woods. So close to where they scalped my brother—"

"Ma! Uncle Abner weren't scalped," I said. "Didn't I tell you, I seen him myself? Those Injuns put him on a horse and stole him away to Canada with the other prisoners."

But Ma weren't listening. She was laying into Pa again. "What do you plan to eat all winter?" she asked. "We should never have left my people."

"We've brought plenty of food." Pa's eyes flashed. Didn't Ma see he were about to lose his temper? "And you know we wore out our welcome. Your people couldn't keep us another winter. Too many mouths to feed, with the men coming home from the war. They wouldn't stand for another."

"Another what?" I asked.

"Another baby," Ma said. She turned to me. "Your pa had no business bringing me here in my condition." She set her hands on her belly.

Her condition? I stared at Pa. His cheeks was red. "Ma's having a baby?" I asked.

Pa cleared his throat. "Yes. You'll have a little brother or sister soon."

I felt stupid. Ma's stout, but she wears so many petticoats and shawls I can't hardly see what she looks like.

"You could have told me," I said. They didn't say nothing, just looked away from me and from each other, too, even though there weren't much to see in that rundown chamber. "Then I guess we better fix the door," I said. "We don't want some wolf marching in while Ma's asleep."

Truth is, I didn't want no wolf sneaking up on me, but I didn't say so.

"True," Pa said. "And tomorrow we'll mend the chimbley. It ain't fit for a fire. Still, we can't complain. They give me the land free, if I promised to set up a store in town. Hannah, you rest on that stump a while. Hiram, come with me. We'll gather wood and build a fire in the clearing to heat the water."

Water. My throat was dry. If only I'd filled the buckets! I followed him outside.

"I'm sorry about this place," Pa told me. "I'll tan the hide of that no-count Mr. Fletcher with his false promises. But where else could we go?"

I shrugged. Ma and Pa had been having this fight since the last full moon.

"Did you find the brook?" Pa asked.

"I did." That much was true. I looked up the hill. The woods was dark, just as Ma said. And if I'd seen an Injun boy—then he must have a family. There might be a whole sight of them, just like in the raid. Would they steal our new baby?

I'd have to go back up the hill. Not just for the water, but to see if that boy was real, or someone chasing me from my bad dreams. I couldn't tell Pa about him yet. Not if I'd conjured him up.

"The buckets are in the shade," I told Pa. True again, though the shade was nowhere near.

"Leave them be," Pa said. "Let's gather wood for a fire.

Your ma will feel right smart if we get a good blaze going. You pick up dry tinder while I find my flint."

I did as he asked, but my eyes strayed to the hill where I'd left the buckets. I couldn't leave them there all day. Would those voices chase after me again? They was almost worse than the real Injun who kidnapped me.

Then I thought of something. If the boy was real, we couldn't stay here. Pa would never make Ma live near no Injuns, would he? Not after they burned our house, kilt our cows. Not after they kidnapped Uncle Abner, stole him away forever. Pa wouldn't do that. Would he?

3. *Daniel*

I came home shamefaced. No fish to show Father, just my empty hands. I spied Rhoda at the foot of the *pompion* patch, but she didn't see me. I slipped past, opened the door, and hurried to the table.

No gifts. Porridge bubbled in the iron pot, but the wide pine boards stood empty.

I slid into my spot on the bench. For my last birthday, Mother made me new moccasins. She stayed up many nights, decorating them with quills and beads. Now they pinched my toes. That same October, Father traded two bushels of rye for a bolt of wool from Boston, and Mother stitched me a warm coat with horn buttons. Where were my gifts today?

Jody's wet nose nudged my hand. I tugged her ears, scratched beneath her chin. "*You* remember my birthday, don't you?"

Her tail swished against my breeches. The shed door opened and Mother came through, a clutch of brown eggs in her hand basket.

"Good morning, Daniel! Thirteen years today," Mother said. She set the eggs down. "May the next year be a fine one."

"Thank you." I smiled. Though she spoke in Pequot, I answered in English. Lately the Pequot words stuck in my throat like the thick porridge she spooned from the pot into my trencher.

"Father was looking for you," she said.

My eyes fell to the table. "I went to catch the trout," I said.

"And did you find him?" She gathered my hair and tied it back with a rawhide twist.

"I did, but he was too swift." I couldn't tell her the rest. It pained her so when Mr. Amidon blamed us for the raid. She'd hate knowing that a boy with a dirty mouth had come to take his place in that tumbled cabin.

"Open the door!" My sister's voice shrilled outside.

I raised the latch. Rhoda stood on the front stoop, arms wrapped around a *pompion* so big, it nearly hid her face.

"Happy birthday!" Rhoda said. "I plucked my best *pompion* just for you."

"Thank you." I hoisted it to my chest. "What a heavy one!"

I set it in the middle of the table. My sister was proud of the seeds she'd set in the ground with Mother this spring, and of their vines snaking through the corn, hiding the orange *pompions* beneath their leaves. I should praise her for this, her biggest one, but I couldn't. A *pompion* was not a true present.

The door flew open on Father, carrying an armload of wood.

"Morning, Daniel." Father strode past me. The wood fell onto the hearth with a clatter. He twisted to look at me as he stirred the fire. "I missed you in the barn."

"I'm sorry, Father." I met his gray eyes with their stern message. "I went looking for the trout. I thought we might eat him for dinner. He's trapped in my fish weir, but he was too swift for me."

"Aye," Father said, "he's a crafty one. Never mind." He touched my shoulder. "Stand up, son."

Did he mean to punish me? I pushed back from the table and held myself tall.

Father set a hand on my head and his eyes looked me up and down. "What do you think, Kate?" he asked. "Is he taller than yesterday?"

My breath came out in a rush and I smiled. So he hadn't forgotten.

"Much taller," Mother said. She looked up from her basketwork. "Soon you will be like twins when you stand side by side."

Twins? I looked up at Father. Neither Rhoda nor I had his

gray eyes or his sandy hair. The neighbors all said we favored Mother.

She must have read my thoughts. "There's more to appearance than coloring," she said. "You've the same square jaw, the same smile." Her fingers twisted the long ash strips back and forth, as if she were braiding Rhoda's hair. "If only my father could see you now. He would be so proud."

"What about me?" Rhoda asked. "Would he be proud of me, too?"

"Of course. 'Tis a shame he's never met you, but we moved before you were born." Mother tugged Rhoda's long braid.

Father turned to stack the logs. He always looks serious when we speak of Mother's people. I wish I could remember our Pequot grandfather, but my first memories are fixed on this hillside.

I returned to my trencher and took a bite of porridge.

"Ready for a birthday surprise?" Father asked.

I glanced at Father's pockets. Was he hiding something?

"'Tis a gift you cannot see," Father said. "It will please you, too, Kate."

I tried to watch his face and not his hands. Father must not think I was greedy.

"What is it?" Rhoda tugged on my sleeve. "Daniel, can you guess?"

"Come, then, Caleb," Mother said. "Don't make us wait."

Father set his hat on the table and smoothed his beard. "After I tended the sheep, I saw smoke coming off the ridge.

I thought it might be a fire—the woods being so dry—so I climbed the hill. And what do you think I found?"

My smile slid away. Father thought this was *good* news?

"We have neighbors," Father said. "A family named Coombs. They moved into that log house, the one the Amidons abandoned after the raid."

The raid. Those two words stilled Mother's hands. Rhoda sidled up beside me on the bench, two fingers in her mouth, but Father didn't notice our quiet.

"They've come from Connecticut with a wagon full of goods," Father said. "They aim to start a store here in town. And Daniel, here's the birthday news. They've a son your age—eleven years old."

"I'm *thirteen* today. That's two years' difference," I said, ashamed of my sharp tongue—but I couldn't help it.

Father looked puzzled. "I thought you'd be glad to have a boy nearby. You've fretted a long time, having no one but a sister to play with."

"Rhoda is a fine playmate." I took my sister's hand. The boy with yellow hair and a twisted mouth could never be my friend. "Did you meet the boy?" I asked.

"No, only his parents." He pointed to my coat, hanging by the door. "Finish your porridge and pull on your warm clothes. I offered to help Mr. Coombs cut timber in their woodlot this morning. We'll do it as changing work. They need to build a shelter for their ox, and we can use extra hands to finish the corn harvest. Their place is nearly in ruins after two years in the weather. Who knows how they'll survive the winter."

The porridge felt heavy in my belly. "Must I help?"

"Of course," Father said. His eyes went from mine to Rhoda's to Mother's. "I misjudged. I thought you'd be pleased to have neighbors on the north side. What's wrong?"

Mother didn't answer, and her dark eyes were grave. The room went so quiet that a pop in the fire made us jump. Finally, she asked, "What will they think of us?"

"If we help them settle in, they will judge us good neighbors," Father said. He laid a hand on Mother's shoulder. "You know the Amidons left because they weren't fit for farming these hills. Don't imagine the worst."

Mother didn't answer. I clenched my fists. So Father hadn't guessed the truth.

"I want to meet the boy," Rhoda said.

"No," I said, and then caught my breath. I hadn't meant to be unkind, but that boy's cruel tongue could wound my sister.

"Why not?" Rhoda crossed her arms. "He could be my friend, too."

"Don't be cross," I said. "Timbering is hard, dirty work."

"Daniel's right." Mother set her basket aside. "Besides, I need your help here. You can gather the rest of the *pompions* and tie up my herbs. You are nearly seven. It's time you learned more about my medicines." Mother lifted some jonnycakes from the iron spider near the hearth and wrapped them in a cloth. "Go on, Caleb. I'll fix some food for the family and send it with Daniel. 'Tis a strange time of year to move, with no garden to harvest. What if they've naught put by for the winter?"

"He claims to have goods to open a store," Father said. "But a dinner basket is a good idea. Be sure there's enough for Daniel and his bottomless belly."

Usually, Father's joshing makes me smile, but not today. I reached for Jody's collar. "I'll bring the dog," I said. "Where's the woodlot?"

"In the stand of oaks, where we hunted turkey this spring," Father said. "You'll hear the saws. Don't be long." He put on his hat and closed the door.

I dug my spoon into the porridge. It had set up cold as river clay, but I forced myself to eat it, rather than hurry up the hill. How could I face that gander-headed boy now?

4. Daniel

As Mother prepared dinner for the new neighbors, I wrapped the laces of my moccasins tight, smoothing the soft deerskin above my ankles. My feet would be cold, working in the woodlot. If only I had tall boots, like Father's, but I didn't dare ask for them. The cobbler hadn't come to Griswold since spring, and the few shillings in Mother's pouch gave a lonesome clink when she shook it.

Rhoda propped her elbows on the table and leaned close to me. "Why won't the new neighbors like us?" she asked.

"Some people don't favor Indians," I said.

"Hsst!" Mother's mouth drew a line as straight as the groove I cut with Father's chisel. "I misspoke," she said. "I'm certain the new neighbors will be fine." She rubbed some russet apples with her apron and set them in the basket. "I was only thinking on the Amidons, who moved away after the raid. You're too young to remember that bad time."

"I am *not*." Rhoda stuck her chin out. "I remember Indians shot people and set houses afire. You carried me to the *sneeksuck,* that dark cave. It smelled sour in there. Daniel came too. We hid all night. Father went with the other men to catch the raiders. I was scared."

Mother set the basket down and came to the bench, pulling Rhoda to her chest. She stroked her head. "I thought you had forgotten." She looked at me over Rhoda's head. "Do you remember?"

"Yes—but I don't like to think on it." The memories are knitted in my mind. I can still hear the gunshots in the valley, still see Timothy, our neighbor, galloping through our gate, yelling that the militia was called up. I remember Father shouting, bidding us to hide, and our dash through the hemlock ravine, where Mother tucked us into a cave. We crouched there all night while musket shots and screams came up the valley. And once, Mother's hand clapped over Rhoda's mouth when a pair of moccasins flashed by, the footsteps hardly making a sound on the wet ground. Moccasins like my own, like Mother's. Two years gone, and I was still trying to puzzle it out.

I looked at Mother now. "We're Indians, yet we ran from Indians," I said.

Rhoda pulled her fingers from her mouth. "Why did they come?" she asked.

"The Caughnawaga people took the part of the British in the war," Mother said. "They came down from Canada to help the British fight the Patriots. Those Indians had naught to do with us. Besides, our war against the Redcoats is over." She took our hands, pulled us to our feet, and pointed to the floor. A shaft of sunshine warmed the chestnut boards. "The sun is smiling this morning. Rhoda, let's finish our chores in the garden." She gave me the basket. "Here's the dinner for our new neighbors. Be sure to welcome them."

Never! I held my tongue, though the word pushed against my lips. I pulled on my hat and coat and stepped outside. Geese flew in two long lines, following the river valley. The birds wobbled, then straightened into a V, like the wake of water fanned out behind a canoe. Their honking made me lonesome. Our own gander answered them from inside the barn, and Jody whimpered.

"The gander says good-bye to the wild geese," Rhoda said.

"The birds feel winter coming," Mother said.

Don't go! I told them. But the geese flew on, their cries growing faint.

"They follow the White River to the Connecticut," Mother said softly in her language. "They fly south, to my people. *Our* people," she said, and pulled us close.

Something twitched in my belly. Mother leaned toward the vanishing flock. I grasped her around the waist, afraid she might fly away with the birds.

"We could build a canoe, and follow them," I said.

"It takes a long time to carve a dugout," Mother said. "Hard work for a boy, and no man to teach you. Your father has never built such a thing."

I pulled away from her. "Father doesn't know Pequot ways, and he hates to make things," I said. More sharp words—had some angry spirit seized me, now I was thirteen?

But Mother surprised me with a laugh. "'Tis true," she said. "Building doesn't always please Caleb—but he does it anyway. How else would we have our barn, our house, and all our fences? It's good you are old enough to help him with the chores of building and running our farm."

"Could *you* teach me to shape a canoe?" I asked.

"Perhaps. But our place is here now." Mother knotted her shawl over her chest. She gave me a little push from behind. "Go on—you'll be late for the changing work."

"Kee-er! Kee-er!" A hawk squealed above us, its tail spread like a fan.

"The red-tailed hawk," Mother said. "A female." She touched Rhoda's head and smiled. "With those hawks, the female is bigger than the male."

The hawk dipped one wing and her red tail feathers caught the sunlight.

"She tells us that someone is coming," Rhoda said.

I stared at my sister. "How do you know?"

"Hawks have *mundtu*," Mother said. "Perhaps this one tells about the new neighbors." She shooed me away. "Go on."

Rhoda squeezed my hand. "Don't be scared," she said.

"I'm not!" But my sister knew me too well. I whistled to Jody and we set off through the corn and across the mowing ground. My nerves prickled all over, as if I'd fallen against an angry porcupine.

5. Hiram

Our fire blazed up soon as we brought Ma some wood. She rested on a stump nearby and fed it twigs while Pa and I unloaded the wagon. We set Ma's rocker near the hearth, then rolled the heavy cider barrels into the corner and piled the sacks and crates on top. Light spilled through chinks in the logs. Pa shook his head. "Look at that. Any self-respecting varmint can slip right in and spoil our grain seeds."

"There ain't much room in this chamber," I said. "Where will the baby sleep?"

"There's time for that yet." Pa wiped his neck with his kerchief and set down on a sack a barley seed. We was both sweating in spite of the frosty air. "Once we get set up in the village, we won't be so crowded in here."

Village? All I'd seen, coming through at dawn, was a few mean houses, some not much better than this one, and the sawmill where Mr. Fletcher worked.

"Pa," I said. "Are we near to our old place?"

"It's a ways downriver, but I still drove Jed all night up the west side a the valley so as not to remind your ma what happened. There's enough bad memories for all of us."

Pa had bad thoughts, too? He started for the door, but I caught his sleeve. "Pa. Did any of them Injuns from the raid stay behind?"

He frowned. "Course not. What gives you that idea? They stole off to Canada with their captives, and our militia too cowardly to follow. Why?"

"Just wondering." I scuffed at the trampled weeds with my boot. I couldn't tell Pa about that boy. Not yet. I weren't sure of him myself. "Pa," I said, soft so Ma wouldn't hear, "do you think Uncle Abner lives?"

"I don't know. He weren't among the slain that morning when the raid was done, and that's a blessing. Still, there weren't nothing left but his ox. We're just lucky that British officer let you and them other boys go; otherwise you'd be in Canada with the savages now."

"Would you have come after me?"

Afore Pa could answer, Ma hailed us from outside. "Isaac? Hiram? What's keeping you?"

"One moment, Hannah." Pa give me a long look. "Your ma has enough worries without you fixing on the raid," he said. "She didn't want to come back up north, so hold your tongue."

I weren't keen on coming to Vermont, either, but did anyone ask me? Course not. As for not thinking on the raid—the more someone says "Don't think on it," the more you do.

We found Ma near the wagon, hoisting our iron kettle. "I need two forked sticks and a long green one, to hold up this pot," Ma said. "That will serve until we fix our hearth." She peered out at me from behind her bonnet. "Hiram, fetch those water buckets and I'll make us some porridge."

"I—I set them in the shade on the hill," I told her.

"Go find them." Ma waved me off and I tucked into the woods. I went as far as a big spruce and studied on my troubles. What should I do? I didn't want to see that Injun again. Still, we needed water. Pa said we'd dig a well soon, but that didn't help today.

What now? Footsteps, and someone whistling—was it the Injun? I ducked behind the tree, but it were just a tall white man, whistling a tune I remembered Ma singing. He come so close I could almost touch him, and he sang, "Where, tell me where, can I find my singing school . . . ?" What strange words were these?

"You'll find it under the tall oak, where the leaves do shake and blow. . . ."

His words was all wrong for that tune, whoever he was. He passed me by without seeing me, then strode right into the clearing like he was on a path he walked every day. Soon as it was safe, I followed after him, running from one tree to the next to stay hid.

No sign of Ma. The two men raised their hats, shook

hands, and talked. Pa pointed every which way: at the house, the clearing, then up the hill. I made myself even smaller behind a big rock. The man didn't stay long. He touched his cap, commenced whistling again, and went off toward the road we'd come up this morning.

When I couldn't see him no more, I run into the clearing. "Pa! Who was that?"

"Our neighbor, Mr. Tucker." Pa was smiling for the first time since we'd come on the cabin. "He stopped over to welcome us. Isn't that fine? He has a family, lives on the next farm."

"Any boys?" I asked.

"One son, and a daughter, too. I didn't ask their ages—he come on me so quick, I didn't think."

Two children. That was good. We could keep watch for the Injun together.

"Mr. Tucker will be back shortly, to help us cut timber for the winter." Pa's eyes fell on my empty hands. "Where is that water?"

"I'm sorry, Pa. I set the buckets down near the brook. And I—I saw a wild animal. It scared me so's I forgot my way back. Could you help me find them?"

"Always a story. Haven't I warned you?"

"It's true, Pa!" Well, almost true. An Injun was a wild animal, wasn't he? I tucked my hands under my armpits, thinking Pa would slap me. Instead, he took me by the elbow and pointed my head toward a big spruce.

"What did I say, at first light?" he said.

"To follow the blazes on the trees, where the last man made a trail."

"Good," Pa said. "Right here is the first blaze. Now run along. No more tall tales or foolishness, and don't come back without those buckets full of water." He let go my arm. "What's got into you? You've been strange ever since we crossed the border a few days back."

Didn't he know? He said he had bad memories, too—but perhaps the noises in my head made me a lunatic, or a fool. I'd best hold my tongue.

"Never mind." Pa's voice surprised me, going all soft. "Who knew we'd be starting all over in the wilderness again, just like last time? I thought for sure things would be more civilized—but I guess the war took its toll up here, too." He nudged me between the shoulders. "Go on now."

I obeyed. Each boot had a millstone's weight as I climbed the hill.

6. Daniel

Mother said hurry to the woodlot. But the track through the timber took me to the brook. How could I cross the brook save on the log Father had cut for that purpose? And how could I cross the log without glancing just once into my pool, to see if my fish weir needed tending, or if Mr. Trout had come back?

A saw rasped high on the hill. Jody swam the brook and

shook herself all over, spraying the red leaves. "Sit," I told her. "Stay." She wagged her tail, watching. The two buckets were tipped over on the far bank. So Gander Head hadn't come back yet. I set the basket down and spied all around. No sign of anyone, and Jody quiet. She'd bark if she smelled that boy.

I lowered myself slow and careful onto the flat stone. As if he'd been waiting for me, Mr. Trout slid from under the roots of the tree. *I won't lose you this time,* I told him, my mouth closed tight. *Gander Head can't catch you. He doesn't even know you're here. Thank you for coming to me.*

I pushed back my coat sleeve, then took off my hat and set it down, slow and careful. I shaped my hat till it was round as Mother's egg basket and held it in one hand while I slid my other arm into the water, lowering it smooth as a greased hinge. My fingers dangled. The skim of ice was gone, but the water still frigid. I didn't move, even when Mr. Trout nibbled my fingertips before returning to the shadows.

I waited, patient. Next time, I was ready. I tickled the trout's belly as Mother had taught me, then scooped him into my hat and tossed him onto the bank, where he twisted and flopped. I scrambled after him and held him tight. His mouth pursed open and closed like a baby bird waiting for food.

"Didn't I say you'd be mine!"

Jody yipped. I held him up to her. "Isn't he fine? Mother will be pleased. Fresh fish for my birthday supper. Thank you, Mr. Trout."

I stunned the fish with a rock, then gathered leaves and ferns to cover him when he stopped struggling. "A leafy shroud," I told him. "I'll fetch you later." I tucked him under a maple root in the deep shade.

Jody barked and I jumped to my feet, took the basket, and, balancing on the log, carried it safe to the other side. I followed the steady *thunk, thunk* of the ax. What had Rhoda said? *Don't be scared.*

I sniffed, smelling fresh sap. Spruce chips littered the ground at my feet and a fresh white blaze bled sap, just at my height. Father had marked the trail for me. Jody's nose snuffled the leaves and she jumped to a run. "Wait," I called, but she was gone to Father. Leaving me to face the new neighbors alone.

The wind came up smart as I climbed the hill. Shouts rang out. Then the crack, the rush of branches, the boom of the tree tumbling. Shiver of the ground under my feet. I waited for the quiet that follows the fall of a big tree, then whistled up Jody. She yipped and hurried to me, tail wagging, as if we'd not been together all morning.

"Good dog." I bent to stroke her ears. "Stay with me."

I peered through a snarl of branches, caught every which way like the twisted tangle of my fish weir. Father spied me and waved. Next to him stood a short man with a soiled waistcoat, but no sign of the yellow-haired boy. I steadied myself and went into the open. The basket weighed heavy on my arm.

"You took a while over your breakfast," Father said. "Say good day to Mr. Coombs."

"Good day," I said and touched my head, finding my hair rather than my hat brim. Fool! I'd left my hat by the brook.

Mr. Coombs held his tongue. His frown sent a shiver into my belly. I knew for certain he was father to the yellow-haired boy. His blue eyes matched Gander Head's. His hair might have been yellow once, but his scalp shone through hair faded as wheat after threshing.

I held up the basket. "My mother sent you some dinner."

Mr. Coombs nodded. "What fine neighbors." His eyes raked over me before he turned to Father. "Your son don't favor you much."

No place to hide. I might have been a mouse in an open meadow, waiting for Rhoda's hawk to catch me in her talons. Then Jody pressed her cold nose in my hand, Father's arm draped over my shoulder, and I could breathe again.

"Lucky for Daniel, his looks match his mother's." I looked up into Father's gray eyes. *Should* a boy favor his father, not his mother? 'Twas not my fault I had Mother's coloring—and hadn't she said that soon Father and I would be twins?

"Unlike me, Daniel is handy with tools," Father said. He let me loose and pointed to the ax, its blade driven into the fresh oak stump. "Ready to limb some branches?"

I nodded and wiggled the ax free of the heartwood. The sap that once fed the oak now oozed out. Perhaps *Cautantowwit* would be angry with me, but I couldn't thank this tree for giving its life. Not if it helped Gander Head. I thought on the turkeys that once roosted in this woodlot, feeding on its acorns, and of how Father and I had hunted here together. Remembered the warm, juicy smell as Mother roasted the gobbler on a spit above the fire. Where would the birds go now?

I hefted the ax and sliced at a small branch, lopping it off.

"My Hiram is clumsy with the ax," Mr. Coombs said.

Hiram. I turned my back to hide my smile. What a funny name. Perfect for someone so buffle brained.

Mr. Coombs wiped his brow with his neckerchief, then retied it above his collar. "I don't know what's happened to the boy. Runs off every time I turn around. I ought to take a strap to him. Sent him for water this morning and he come back empty-handed, saying he saw some wild animal. Always a story, some foolish excuse."

Wild animal? Was that what he'd called me? Heat rushed into my face. And then Jody barked and ran into the heavy timber. I caught a flash of yellow before Gander Head ducked behind a tree, his hands over his head.

"Call off your dog!" Gander Head yelled.

I set to my chopping, striking the branches with all my force as if I hadn't heard him. Jody barked louder and Father whistled sharp. Jody trotted back to us, but the fur on her neck still bristled and I tucked away a smile. Didn't Father say that Jody could smell trouble from miles away?

"Hiram, where you been?" Mr. Coombs said.

"Ma told me to fetch some feed for the ox."

Was this a tall tale, too? I gripped the ax, felt the heft of its weight, the bite of its blade, which Father had honed on the whetstone yesterday. I watched that ugly boy from behind the branches of the downed oak. He hadn't seen me yet.

"Say good day to our new neighbors," Mr. Coombs said. "This is Mr. Tucker and his son, Daniel."

I stepped out from behind the tree. Gander Head's face went blotchy, like a dappled mare.

"Morning," Gander Head said. He shook Father's hand. Glanced at me, back at Father. I could read his face clear as the letters Rhoda and I write on our slates. He couldn't puzzle out how a sandy-haired, pink-complexioned man like Father could have a boy like me. Had he no sense?

Gander Head sneered at me, then looked at my ax. A muscle twitched in his cheek, but he didn't move.

"Let's get back to work." Mr. Coombs picked up the two-man saw. "Hiram, Daniel is limbing up trees. You can haul brush into the pile we started. Mr. Tucker and I will saw the trunks into cordwood."

Hiram's mouth twisted, like a dog with a mean snarl. He took two steps back from his father. "I ain't working with no dirty Injun," he said.

He bolted.

My hands trembled so I feared I'd drop the ax.

"Hiram!" Mr. Coombs yelled. "You're in for a licking."

Gander Head disappeared; the forest swallowed him up. I could have told Mr. Coombs his son was a coward, yellow as his hair, but I held my tongue.

Now Mr. Coombs had the mottled face. "The boy owes you an apology, Mr. Tucker," he said. "I don't know what to do with him."

"Daniel is owed the apology," Father said, his voice like cold iron.

"Fair enough. I guess you surprised us both, having a son so dark when you're right fair—that's all. We don't want no trouble." Mr. Coombs looked at me, though I could tell he'd rather not. "I'm sorry for what my boy said."

Was he? I couldn't tell. Mr. Coombs didn't meet my eyes. I set the ax down, ready to bolt myself.

"Daniel's mother, my wife, is a full-blood Pequot, and the local doctress," Father said. "Most folks in Griswold speak highly of her. She's saved many lives here, including my own."

"How's that?" Mr. Coombs asked.

Father rubbed his beard. His eyes slid over to me and I tried to warn him: *Don't tell our story to a stranger!* But he went right on. I found Jody's silky ear and stroked it for comfort.

"I nearly drowned back in Connecticut, knocked senseless into the Thames River during the spring rush," Father said. "The current carried me downstream. My wife's family was fishing, and I got tangled in their fish weir."

Father smiled. When he told this story at home, Mother always said, "We were fishing for shad, not men." But Mr. Coombs kept a sober face as Father went on. "My wife's brother and father pulled me out. For days, I didn't know where I was, or who I was." He smiled. "Kate nursed me back to health, and we married—although neither family wished it."

Neither family wished it? I'd never heard that part of the story. Would Father tell this man all our private doings? I feigned a cough and Father seemed to read me, because he hefted his end of the saw. "We'd best keep on. I have other chores at home."

"We don't mean no harm," Mr. Coombs said. "We hail from Connecticut, too—perhaps we were neighbors there, long ago." He had the look of Jody, when I catch her with her nose in the milk pail. He hoisted his end of the saw. "I'm grateful for the changing work. We'll pay you back when you need help."

Father's eyes caught mine. "You all right with that ax?"

Of course I was. Still, I felt the kindness in his voice. Imagined the words he might have said: *I'm sorry for this, son.*

I hoisted the ax again and stepped close to the oak. It sprawled like a fallen man, lying with his arms and legs in the air. I raised the ax, swung it hard, let it drop. *Thwack!* The blade sliced through a small branch. *Thwack!* I lopped it off. *Thwack!* I struck at a bigger limb. Sap oozed from the wound. The branch fell away, like an arm severed from a shoulder bone.

Take that. And that. And that.

7. Hiram

I run fast as I could, dodging right, then left, in case Pa tried to come after me. The woods got dark and thick. I stopped, put my head down, and coughed up something messy looking. When I got my breath, I seen two things. One, no Pa coming after me. And two, I was plumb lost.

I cussed awhile, but it didn't do me no good. I found the sun, the way Pa showed me, but what was the use? We just moved here. I don't know where the sun falls over the house yet. So I waited until I was breathing slow and quiet. Then I heard the saw going, and the chop of that Injun's ax, so I weren't too far from home.

The ax! The Injuns who stole Uncle Abner and took me away from Ma carried axes; spears, too. And they scalped our neighbor, peeled his skin right off with a hatchet. I shook my head hard to rid my mind of that sight. Anyway, that Injun boy might be taller than me, but he was bony as an old plucked chicken. He couldn't hurt Pa, could he? Not with his own pa beside him.

That set me thinking. How did Mr. Tucker, white as my own ma, get a son looks like an Injun? I rapped my head with my knuckles. Fool. Course. His ma must be an Injun. So he was a dirty half-breed. In fact, he didn't look like half of anything to me. More like a full Injun and just as ornery.

The chopping sounds quit and I heard water trickling, not too far off. I followed the sound to the stream and found my buckets, sitting where I left them, but tipped on their sides. Had he fooled with them? I peeked inside: nothing there. I picked one up and dipped it into the pool, where I saw something strange. A funny dam sat under the water, sticks and twigs woven together, like a wattle fence. Had the Injun boy made this? I set the full bucket down and then I seen something else: a log felled over the brook to make a bridge. And on the other side, setting in the sun beside the big tree, the Injun boy's hat.

I balanced acrost that log with my arms out so I wouldn't fall in, and picked up the hat. Whew. What a smell. Cooking smoke from an Injun's fire—

But wait—what was this? Sunshine lit up a fishtail right beside my foot, sticking out from under a tree root. I dropped the hat, knelt down, and yanked. Sure enough, it was the big brown trout. So he'd caught it after all. Wrapped it in ferns to keep it fresh, pushed it under the roots—but left the tail in plain sight. Now who was buffle brained? I held the fish up against my arm. He was a big one, all right. With his tail touching my elbow, his jaw reached my fingertips.

"Ain't you a fine fish! Ma will be pleased," I told that trout. "If I play it right, she'll think I caught you myself. Maybe she'll forget I'm late with the water."

I covered him with the ferns, carried him back acrost the log, and set him in the empty bucket. 'Fore I left, I grabbed the Injun's ugly hat, tossed it into the pool, and poked it with a long stick. It sank to the bottom. I laughed. "That will show you."

I hurried back to the clearing. The water from the brimming bucket slopped all over my britches, but I didn't care. I found Ma setting outside on a stump, her arms wrapped around her belly like she was trying to keep that baby from falling out.

When she turned to look at me, her face was red as her hair. Trouble.

"Where you been?" she said. "I hailed you for a long time."

"I brought you a surprise." I set the full bucket down first, then lifted the fish and laid it in her lap, all wrapped in ferns like I'd done him up myself. "Look! Ain't he a beauty?"

She smiled. I swear, I'd done forgot she could be pretty sometimes. She pulled off those ferns and held him up.

"Aren't you smart?" she said. "How'd you catch him?"

I was ready for that question. "Caught him in the bucket," I told her. "He was sluggish. Guess he don't move so fast in the cold—though he put up a fuss. I had to be quick to hold on to him."

She didn't even make a face, so she must have believed me. She picked at my hair. "Look at you. Full of twigs. Clean yourself up while I gut this fish. We'll have it ready for your pa when he comes in for dinner. Won't he be surprised?"

8. Daniel

I limbed branches and hauled brush all morning. When the sun crossed the noon mark, I swung the ax into a stump and watched it shiver in the hardwood. My shoulders and back needed some of Mother's salve and my belly growled loud as Jody when she comes on the scent of a she-bear.

Father laughed and set down the saw. "I hear your empty belly," he said. "Must be past noon."

I held my tongue, fearing what must come next.

"We'll bring your dinner basket to the house," Mr. Coombs said, "as long as you don't mind the conditions."

"Never mind; we won't trouble your wife," Father said, but Mr. Coombs pressed us to join him. I had to choose: leave my belly empty, or face Gander Boy again. My belly won, so I started after Father, my steps heavy in the dry leaves. Jody made a zigzag path in front of me, her nose close to the ground.

I patted her head. "You smell that old gobbler we tried to catch, don't you?" I watched for turkey feathers but didn't see any. Felling those oaks, we stole the gobbler's fall food. If only the Coombses had never come to Griswold!

Smoke drifted our way as we came into the open. The little log house was shabby and lonesome in the clearing. Brush grew up around the stumps and the chimney pitched sideways, like a tree feeling the final cut of the saw. A woman leaned over a fire. Her face was red as the rusty curls poking from her bonnet. No sign of Gander Boy.

I stopped. My mouth watered. I smelled hot fat—and something else.

The woman straightened, set the skillet on a stump, and stared at us. I stared right back, only half seeing the woman, her belly round as Rhoda's *pompion,* her fingers poking from strange white gloves, her eyes peering at me as if she needed Father's spectacles.

What held my gaze was the skillet and the trout—Mr. Trout—*my* trout!—sizzling in fat. The fish lay open in the pan, his pink flesh already white in the heat, head gone.

I clenched my fists. A roaring sound filled my head, a rush like water after the ice breakup in the spring, and I couldn't hear anything else. *He stole it! My trout. Mine, that I caught for my birthday supper. Mine!*

Father's voice came from far away. "Daniel, did you hear me? Say good day to Mrs. Coombs."

I stepped forward. "That's my trout. I caught him myself."

"I beg your pardon." The woman gave me a look of poison.

I stepped close to the fire. Hot grease spat at my breeches, but I didn't flinch. "I built a fish weir to trap him in our brook. I watched him every day. Mended the weir so he couldn't escape. Today I snatched him up with my bare hands and wrapped him in ferns so he wouldn't spoil. If you go to my hiding place, you'll find him gone."

I caught my breath. I hadn't meant to give a speech as long as a sermon. The woman's eyes darted to her husband and I saw she guessed: I told the truth.

Mr. Coombs cleared his throat and tried to smile. "So Daniel is a storyteller, too," he said.

"I don't lie. He's mine!" I reached for the skillet.

"Daniel!" Father caught my hand. "You'll burn yourself."

"Hannah, can you explain?" Mr. Coombs asked.

"Certainly." Mrs. Coombs stepped closer and fixed her cold blue eyes on Father. "Hiram caught this trout in our bucket and fetched it home," she said. "Seeing you're so neighborly with the changing work, we're happy to share it with you and your—your Indian boy."

Father's smile was as icy as Mrs. Coombs's. "Daniel is my *son*. He would not tell a falsehood," he said. I was glad for the way he said *son,* but his next words hit me full in the belly. "I'm certain Daniel will share his fish. The brook marks the boundary, so we must divide its water and the fish that live there." Father's grip on my shoulder told me I should hold my tongue. "Perhaps we can catch another trout before the cold comes on."

"He was the biggest one," I said, pulling away. "I built the weir just for him." How could Father not understand?

Mr. Coombs took off his cap and rubbed his thin hair until his scalp shone through. "Where is Hiram, anyway? Seems we need to hear his side of the story." He cupped his hands around his mouth. "Hiyyy-ram!"

Squirrels chattered, answering him back, and Jody whimpered.

"Perhaps he felt shy when he saw we had company," Mrs. Coombs said.

Gander Head, shy? I dug my nails into my palms to keep me silent. So far, nothing good had come of my birthday.

"Let's not disagree," Father said. "'Tis no way to begin being neighbors." He hoisted our basket. "My wife sent you dinner. We'll eat it with the trout."

"That's a kindness." Mrs. Coombs took the basket and held it up. "What lovely handwork." She turned it this way and that. Sunlight fell on the alternating patterns of black and white, and on the flowers Mother had painted on so carefully. "Isaac, look at this design," she said. "Perhaps we should offer these in our store."

I spoke up again. I couldn't help myself. "My mother made it," I told her. "She sells her baskets to the neighbors, and Mr. Shaw takes them to Boston."

"Is that so?" Mrs. Coombs's smile faded as she set the basket down. She brushed her hands—as if Mother's basket were filthy!

Hiram's mother had never met mine, yet already she hated her. Enough of this. When Father and Mr. Coombs bent over the bucket to wash their hands, I slipped into the deep shadows of the timber.

Dry leaves crunched behind me. I whirled around, but 'twas only Jody. "Good dog." I knelt and caught her close, rubbing my cheek against her silky ear. "You left the wicked people behind, didn't you?" Her tail swished in the leaves. I set her free and hurried home, even though my belly clenched tight, begging for food. I crossed the brook, stopped in the pool of sunshine where I'd left my hat—and saw nothing.

Had he stolen my hat, too? I might catch another fish, as Father said—though none so big as Mr. Trout—but I'd not find a hat as warm as this one.

I leaned over the pool. My own reflection stared back, brown cheeks almost as dark as the water. Was that a rock on the bottom, or something else? I found a long stick and poked at the streambed, feeling stones, muck—and then something soft. I caught hold and brought the hat up. The heavy felt was sodden, but it would dry.

I carried it across the meadow ground, into the cornfield, over the *pompion* vines. Though Father would scold me, I clapped my hands to spook the sheep in their pen and laughed when they ran, then huddled in the corner. Jody barked.

But wait—what was this?

A strange white horse stood near the gate, its reins dangling in the dirt. The horse so thin, its hipbones stuck out like staves in an unfinished barrel. I stepped toward it, then stopped.

A wail came from the house. A scream, another wail.

Mother? Rhoda?

The screams came again and I crouched behind the rotting chestnut stump, my heart galloping. Was Mother in trouble? Or Rhoda hurt?

I should go inside. I knew I should. But I covered my ears and curled up in a ball behind the stump, trembling.

I lay still a long time, until Jody whimpered and her tongue scraped at my hand. Then Rhoda chattered in the house like a chipmunk running for its nest and I scrambled to my feet, ashamed. Nothing was amiss. I brushed off my jacket.

Someone must be visiting, perhaps a neighbor with a strange ailment who had surprised Mother.

The horse whickered and stamped a foreleg as I came close. "Easy." I peeked beneath the belly. 'Twas a mare. I stroked her neck. "You're a tired old girl, aren't you."

Two bundles rested on the ground beside her. The red pelt of *A'waumps* lay across the top bundle, its fur so full I thought, for a moment, the fox was still alive. I stroked the soft pelt and turned it over. Its body had been hollowed into a quiver, holding four arrows tipped with turkey feathers.

Pequot arrows. Who was here?

I thought of the hawk circling and of Rhoda saying, *Someone is coming.* Did my sister have second sight?

I pushed the door open. Mother stood near the hearth in our front chamber. Her cheeks were wet and her hands flew up and down, fast as a hummingbird's wings. Pequot words tumbled from her mouth. She spoke to someone, wrapped in a blanket, who had the bony look of the old horse outside. Was it a man or a woman?

"Daniel!" Rhoda spied me and ran over, grabbing my hands as if we were to dance. "Grandfather is here!"

Grandfather? "But how—"

The blanket stirred. A gray braid, long as Mother's, fell over an old man's shoulder. He turned to me. Black eyes glittering like polished stones. A face weathered as old deerskin. Empty spots where teeth were missing. My eyes fell to my feet.

"Daniel," Mother said in her language. "Say hello to your grandfather."

My throat felt tight, as if I'd swallowed a mess of fish bones. "Grandfather," I said. The Pequot word tasted of rust, I'd used it so seldom. "Welcome."

The old man stood slowly and came to me. He cupped his hands around my skull. "Grandson." His voice was dry and raspy as old leaves and his breath was stale as he spoke words I didn't understand. I found Mother's eyes, huge and dark in her startled face.

"He says that you have the look of another Daniel, from long ago, named *Neesouweegun*—who was a *powwaw*," she said.

A *powwaw*? I pulled away. How could he say this of me?

"But he doesn't know me," I told Mother, in English this time.

"I see it in your eyes," Grandfather said. Now *he* spoke English, too.

I flushed, ashamed. So he understood me. Never mind. I would not be a medicine man, no matter what he said. And didn't Mother complain that the old ways were sliding away, like current slipping down the river? I held so still I could hear my own blood rushing inside me.

Grandfather's face softened. "It's true I don't know you well. That is why I have come." He threw off his blanket and adjusted a wooden cup strapped to his deerskin belt. "You can help me with my horse." He was stooped, but his step was strong as he passed me by. His moccasins made no sound.

I watched him go outside. "Mother, were you surprised?"

She nodded. "Completely. Remember the hawk this morning? We felt her *mundtu,* but I never dreamed she foretold a visit from my father."

"I said someone was coming," Rhoda reminded us.

"Yes. And you were right," Mother said.

I went outside. The old man waited for me on the doorstep. "Today is your birthday," he said.

"You remembered?"

"Of course. You were born in October, when the geese flew south. They have flown thirteen times since you were born. It was time I came."

He went to his horse and I followed. His words about the *powwaw* made me wary. Could Grandfather cast a spell on me? Could he speak my future, without my consent? No. He couldn't make me a *powwaw* against my will. Could he?

We led the old mare into the barn and shut her in an empty stall. I rubbed her down with a rag while thoughts both knitted and unraveled in my mind. Father said I favored Mother. Grandfather said I had the look of a *powwaw.* Mother said that soon Father and I would be like twins. Did each person see a different Daniel when they looked on me?

I felt as penned in as Grandfather's mare, pawing the floor and butting her nose against the empty manger.

9. Hiram

I come out from the woods soon as that boy run from the clearing.

"Where you been?" Pa asked.

"I found the old privy," I said. Pa's eyes told me he didn't believe me, but he stayed quiet. What could he say, with Mr. Tucker sitting right there on a stump, eating from our trencher?

That fish tasted sweet and juicy, but I couldn't hardly swallow, wondering if Pa would whup me later. While we finished the jonnycake and crunched on apples from the basket, I stole looks at Mr. Tucker. An ugly scar ran acrost his forehead. I wanted to ask if an Injun had tried to scalp him, but I held my tongue.

"I shouldn't tarry," Mr. Tucker said when we was done.

"We'd best get back to the timbering," Pa said. "We appreciate your help, don't we, Hannah?" He gave Ma a long look, but she didn't say nothing.

Mr. Tucker cast a sad glance over our cabin. "You have a sore lot of work ahead of you," he said. "We're only a small settlement, but the neighbors help each other when we can. Send word to Mr. Fletcher if you want to gather folks to mend your roof or dig a well."

Ma's laugh was scornful. "I won't be speaking to Mr. Fletcher anytime soon."

"Hannah," Pa warned, but there weren't no stopping Ma. Didn't he know that?

"Mr. Fletcher promised us a decent house and a real village where townsfolk need a store," Ma said. "Instead, they give us a pigsty. We turned our ox into the only chamber to graze. As for the village, I saw just a few houses, hardly enough to warrant a store. No proper meetinghouse for prayers, no school for Hiram, nothing."

Since when did she plan on sending me to school? That was news to me.

Mr. Tucker cleared his throat. Probably aiming to be polite when he wished to be gone. For an instant, Ma made me right ashamed.

"'Tis true, we're not much of a town yet," Mr. Tucker said. "But traveling parsons come by from time to time to read us a sermon. The Vermont Republic has a constitution now. It bids every town to start a school, so we plan to build one next year. I've heard a cooper is setting up shop across the White River. Now the war is over, we can live without fear."

Was I the only one left who remembered what happened in the war? A funny thought buzzed like a skeeter in my head. If Mr. Tucker was married to an Injun, was he part of the raid that took Uncle Abner? I shifted from foot to foot, wishing he'd go along.

"And what about a doctor?" Ma asked. Pa set a hand on her arm but she kept right on. "As you can see, Mr. Tucker, I'll be needing one before too long."

Pa's face colored all the way to his bald dome, but Mr. Tucker didn't seem flustered. "You're in luck," Mr. Tucker said. "As I told Mr. Coombs this morning, my wife, Kate, is an Indian doctress. She can care for you when your time comes. And she has good neighbor women to help you."

An Indian doctress? Who ever heard of such a thing?

"Why, that's right kind of you——" Pa said, but Ma spoke sharp again.

"We need a real doctor," she said.

You should a seen Mr. Tucker's face then. His scar turned a funny color, like a night crawler stuck on a fishhook. "My wife has caught hundreds of babies, both here and in Connecticut, with nary a bit of trouble," he said. "But you suit yourself."

"We'll do that," Ma said. She took up her skillet and turned her back on us.

Mr. Tucker hoisted his basket and headed to the woodlot without saying good-bye. I watched Ma and Pa. What was all that fuss about? And what did Mr. Tucker mean, *catching* a baby? Do they toss it around like a ball? Maybe the men feel funny talking about babies, the way I do.

"Hannah," Pa said. "You'd best be more friendly, when we don't know a soul in this place. The Tuckers came here from Connecticut, same as we did."

"Not from our part of Connecticut," Ma said. "I promise you that."

Pa sighed and put on his hat. "Come with us, Hiram. No more running off, you hear?"

"Yes sir," I said.

"Wait—let him stay with me." Ma reached out her hand to Pa and he helped her to standing. She kept one hand on her back. "I'd like some help making a proper bed. That mud floor will pain me all over."

Pa looked me up and down. "If I leave you with the hatchet, can you cut your ma some hemlock boughs? No foolishness," he said, and touched his belt. I knew what that meant, though Pa talked about whupping me more than he took up the strap. He passed the hatchet over real slow. "No daydreaming."

"Yes, Pa," I said.

I was glad he left me behind, but I changed my mind after I seen what Ma wanted me to do. First she showed me which trees was hemlock. "The soft ones with feathery branches," she said. "They'll make a nice pallet until we have a real bed tick."

I weren't used to the hatchet and my hands got sore, chopping enough branches to make Ma happy. I hauled them to the cabin and helped her pile them on the dirt floor. We took her quilt out from the wagon and spread it over the boughs. It weren't very smooth, but she still thanked me.

"Oh," Ma said, very sudden. She held on to her belly and bit her lip. "This baby kicks something fierce. I'd better lie down."

I was skairt for sure. "Is it coming out? Shall I get Pa?"

"No," Ma said. "Just help me settle."

I held her hands while she set herself down on the quilt.

She was so heavy I nearly fell over backward helping her. Ma's cheeks went white, and her belly stuck up when she lay on her back.

"The baby looks big," I told her. "How does it get out?"

"Hiram Coombs! Shame on you!" Ma slapped my leg hard. She could a lit a fire with her eyes. "That Mr. Tucker is a fool. I'd never let some Injun doctress help me with my baby." Her eyes narrowed to slits. "You keep away from them," she said. "Now fetch my shawl. I'm tuckered out."

Time I found the shawl amongst the cotton bales, Ma was already asleep. I laid the shawl over her and tiptoed away fast.

Outside, I picked up the empty buckets, figuring to fill them again and make Ma happy. By now, my feet knew the way by themselves, and when they reached the brook, those feet just made me set the buckets down, balance acrost that log, and keep going. Part of me wanted to obey Ma and Pa, while the other part said: *Go. See who they are. Make sure they don't mean harm to Ma or the baby.*

The track on the other side was worn smooth. That Injun boy must come up here every day. The woods was dark for a bit; then I saw daylight and a meadow ground. I hid behind a big pine tree at the edge of their clearing.

The Tuckers' place was right smart compared to ours. They had sheep in a pen, a cornfield, and a big meadow ground with wheat stubble poking up. The house even had clapboards, a straight stone chimbley, and a barn for their animals. Not a soul outside, so I run down into the cornfield, ducking in and out a the dried stalks. They rustled in the wind. Maybe no one would hear my footsteps. I hid behind a big haycock near the barn.

Just in time. The door opened and that Daniel boy come out. I scrunched up small and didn't breathe. And who do you think was behind him? A full-blood Injun chief, that's who.

My eyes must a bugged right out, I stared so hard. That chief had gray hair down his back, a blanket over his shoulder, and some shiny jewelry dangling on his bare chest. He leaned over and picked up this fox skin laying on the ground, full of Injun arrows. He pulled one out and showed it to the boy. Those arrowheads looked sharp enough to put your eye out. A tomahawk dangled from the quiver, making me think of our neighbor what was scalped in the raid. My teeth begun to chatter, but I couldn't move.

The old chief said some strange words to Daniel. They didn't make no sense to me, but Daniel made a few of those same funny sounds, too.

The old man must a told Daniel to carry his things inside, because he picked up one of the bundles. Soon as they had their backs to me, I stood up nice and slow. I thought I could get away, but their dog come flying out the house, snarling and barking and growling. I backed up against the fence and kicked at her.

"Git off a me!" I yelled. "Git!"

The old Injun whistled at the dog, but she didn't pay him no mind. Her fur stuck up all around her collar. I kicked at her again and missed. The Injun hurried over and grabbed that dog by the collar, talking quiet to her, before he come up to me. His mouth twitched like he might laugh.

"Git away!" I told him. "Leave me be!"

That old Injun gives me a toothy smile and reached his hand out. "Don't be afraid, Yellow Hair," he said.

So he talked English, too. And who was Yellow Hair? Me? I scrambled onto the fence, looking every which way. Next thing, a little Injun girl hurries onto the front step. Right behind her was a woman with a dark face and hair all the way to her apron sash. Injuns everywhere! They all stared at me. Daniel set down his bundle. His ma touched his shoulder and talked more of those strange words. They sounded like scolding. Daniel didn't pay her no mind. He strutted right over to me and stood beside the chief.

"Where do you live, Yellow Hair?" the chief asked me. Up close, he looked even older than I thought. His face was hard and dry and his eyes was fierce. A shiny knife hung at his waist.

"My name is Hiram, not Yellow Hair," I told him. My heart jumped like a thirsty frog headed for a pond. "Don't touch me," I said. "Hey!"

Daniel shoved me! I tumbled off the fence and landed on my backside in a mess of sheep dung. Even worse, a gander come running at me from inside the barn, hissing like a snake. I scrambled into the corner. Which way to go?

Daniel covered his mouth. He was laughing and the old man spoke to him sharp.

"You pushed me!" I yelled at Daniel. "You're dirty In-juns—all a you!"

I turned my back on the whole mess of them, scrambled over the fence, and run. Every few feet, I snatched a look at the old man over my shoulder. He didn't touch the knife, or his arrows, but still I pulled my hat down tight against my neck. If he shot me with one a those arrows, maybe it would bounce off.

What a buffle brain! Hadn't I seen what those arrows could do in the raid? Pierce a man's chest right to his heart? I whistled that "Yankee Doodle" fife tune, the one the Con-necticut regiment played going to fight the Tories, but it didn't work. The other noises was already starting in my head.

Cows bawling. Women screaming. Uncle Abner roaring when they stabbed his leg. Hoofbeats rumbling. The Injun's arm tight around my waist. The hawk, diving down and chasing me through the woods when I escaped. The raid happening all over again.

I ran, but the noises followed me straight to the brook. I fell down for a drink, then closed my eyes and waited till it was quiet. When the brook's steady trickling pushed the other sounds away, I filled my buckets and went home.

The water slopped over my britches and I smelled like a barnyard. Never mind. I had no time to waste. Pa had to know about this. We couldn't live near a mess of Injuns. What if Ma was right, and they scalped Uncle Abner for his red hair? They could scalp Ma, too.

I come out in the open. The fire was cold and the clearing quiet. Jed pulled at his rope, nibbling some brush. I set the buckets down. "Pa!" I called. "Ma!"

I hurried to the house. When Pa heard this news, he'd be too upset to whup me. He'd pack our things and we'd head back to Connecticut before the sun even set. I'd never set eyes on that Injun family again.

Least, that's what I hoped.

10. Daniel

I stood still, waiting, until that ugly yellow head disappeared into the timber.

"Daniel. What ails you?" Mother called from the fore-yard.

I studied the ground. Grandfather stepped back from me, waiting.

"Come to the house," Mother said.

My feet weighed heavy and I couldn't meet her dark eyes, so disapproving.

"Is that the new boy?" Rhoda asked. "Why did you push him? What did he say?"

"Never mind." I was glad she'd not come close enough to hear. "He's full of malice." I durst not say more, for fear of hurting her.

"Did you push him off the fence?" Mother asked.

I couldn't lie; Grandfather had seen me. "Yes," I told her.

"*Nuk.* I did." My eyes burned. "He spoiled my birthday! All of it."

"'Tis no way to behave, birthday or not," Mother said. "Why would you do such a thing?"

If she'd heard Hiram's words, perhaps she'd not scold me—but still I held my tongue.

Grandfather set a hand on my shoulder. "What did Yellow Hair call himself?"

"Hiram," I said. "Hi—rum."

Rhoda laughed. "*Hi,* boy. Want some *rum?*"

"Enough foolishness," Grandfather said, and Rhoda's lip trembled. I took her hand.

"Help me with my things," Grandfather said. He hoisted one of his bundles and went inside.

"Here, Rhoda," I said. "Fetch *A'waumps.* Feel his softness."

She brushed her eyes, lifted the fox quiver and stroked its fur, then followed after Grandfather.

Mother sank onto the stone step, blocking my way. "Stay a minute." She looked toward the mountains. I followed her gaze. The clear sky meant Jack Frost would bite hard again this night. "You must not treat the boy badly," Mother said. "He's a stranger here."

"But he—"

"Ssst. Listen. When we first came to Griswold, we were one of just six families getting settled. One was Mr. Chase, the blacksmith. He shunned us at first. Tried to drive us away. He said cruel words about the Pequot people."

"Mr. Chase?" I was surprised. "But he's our friend."

"Yes," Mother said. "He is now. Our first autumn here, Mr. Chase burned himself at his forge. I fixed him a poultice of linseed and cowslip and doctored him for many weeks. Now he sings my praises to everyone, but it wasn't always so." She sighed and regarded me again. "His early coldness left a scar inside me like the one on his hand. 'Tis always better to welcome a new family."

I shifted from foot to foot. If I told Mother the truth about Hiram, it could give her another scar. Yet if I didn't, she would expect me to be friendly, to welcome him. And I couldn't do that. I thought of Mrs. Coombs and her cold eyes raking over me. 'Twas a blessing Mother hadn't seen that.

She shivered and stood up. "I must finish the garden before nightfall. Go on; help your grandfather settle in. He can sleep in the back chamber." She disappeared among the cornstalks.

I hoisted Grandfather's heavy bundle and stumbled under its weight. Something rattled as I carried it to the small chamber where Mother kept her herbs, roots, and medicines.

"Wegun," Grandfather said. "It's good to be here." He padded across the room, soft as a cat on field grass. He fingered a bundle of dried roots on Mother's shelf. Picked up a finished basket. Held her wampum bracelet to the light and made a grunting sound.

"I gave her this when she was a girl," he said in Pequot. "I'm glad she kept it." He looked through the small window, then pointed to the tangled pile of ash splints in the corner. "My pallet belongs here," he said. "We need to move the wood."

I found Rhoda's eyes. Would Mother mind? We did as the old man asked, gathering the long strips. They rattled and clacked as we stacked them beneath the shelves. We spoke in English, and I was glad. I didn't speak Pequot as smoothly as Mother did or even as well as Rhoda.

"May I open your bundle?" Rhoda asked.

Grandfather nodded. Rhoda's thin fingers struggled with the tight rawhide knots.

"Here." I pushed her hands away. "Let me."

"Wait!" Rhoda whined.

"No fighting." The old man's bark was like Jody's. I sat on my hands to keep them still. Rhoda was so slow! She took a sharp piece of bone from Grandfather and pried it into the knots, loosening them one at a time.

The skin fell open with a jingle-jangle. Inside I found a blanket full of clothes, a flint for starting fires, a clay pipe, a tobacco pouch, and a red rattle. We both grabbed for the rattle, but Rhoda reached it first. "Let me try." She shook it, laughing at its soft hissing sound.

"This is not for you," Grandfather said, and took the rattle away. "It is meant only for healing ceremonies."

Rhoda's lip quivered. She stuck her fingers in her mouth. 'Twas unfair to make my sister sad again! Grandfather didn't seem to notice. I pulled her close. "Look at this skin," I said, and turned over the thick pelt that had made the bundle.

The fur was black as Rhoda's eyes. I lifted it to my nose, but the scent didn't speak to me. What was it?

Rhoda's fingers sank into the deep fur. "Is it a bear?" she asked.

"No—a wolf," the old man said.

"But wolves are gray," Rhoda said.

Mother stood in the door, holding a basket of onions. She looked at the skin. "Black wolves are rare. I remember when you received it," she told Grandfather. "You had cured a woman with a bad disease."

"Someone gave this to you?" I asked.

"Yes," Grandfather said. "I danced and sang to banish an illness. If someone is sick and the *powwaw* cures them, a black wolf skin is a worthy gift."

Powwaw. The word felt as heavy as the skin itself. Grandfather's eyes seemed to sink into my skull. "The *mundtu,* the power that made me a *powwaw,* falls down before white man's diseases," Grandfather said. "My skill has grown weak." He swayed a little.

Mother cupped her hand under Grandfather's elbow. "You found your way to us," she said. "Hundreds of miles. Some power guided you."

Grandfather grunted. "I received your messages through Abenaki traders," he said. "They told me where you are living. But I didn't know it was a trip of so many days. I ran out of *nocake,* the last parched corn of our harvest. Then I lived on squirrels and fish."

"Never mind," Mother said. "You came, and we're glad."

She pressed her hand against Grandfather's cheek, then left the chamber, with Rhoda behind her.

So my grandfather caught fish, too. I thought on Mr. Trout. If I told Grandfather how Gander Head stole my fish, would he understand why I'd pushed him?

Grandfather opened another bundle. "How do you know if something has *mundtu?*" I asked him. "Can you feel it?"

He sighed. "This is not the time for lessons. Maybe later, when I have rested." He lifted a wool shirt from the bundle, then a pair of breeches.

A wooden club with a carved head rolled from the deer-skin bundle. I caught it and lifted it up. "What is this?" I asked.

"A war club," Grandfather said. "It was my father's."

'Twas heavier than an ax, the round head smooth and shiny as a wet otter.

"Did you use it in a war?" I asked.

"No. Those days were gone in my father's time, and this club is worthless against guns. I was too old to join in the war of the Revolution, although the Pequot people rose with the Patriots against the Redcoats."

I hadn't known that. "Some Indians fought *with* the Redcoats," I said. "They came down from Canada and kidnapped people, stole them away. Mother hid us in a *sneeksuck,* a river cave."

"Yes, she told me about that raid. But the war is over now."

I sighed. That was what everyone always said, but what about the burned farms, and the captives who never came back? Grandfather returned to his unpacking and I touched his elbow. "If someone fought you now, would you hit him with the war club?" I asked.

"Perhaps." Grandfather laughed, a soft raspy sound like a saw cleaving wet wood. "I know why you ask. This is not for you to use against Yellow Hair."

I stared at the floor. How could he know my mind? Perhaps his *mundtu* was strong after all. Grandfather set the club in the corner. "I will need some pegs or nails to hang my clothes," he said.

I hesitated. "Father says Mr. Chase's iron nails are precious."

"Two will be enough," Grandfather said.

So he *was* staying. I went to the barn for the nails and a hammer. I should be happy, but instead, the news twisted and squirmed in my empty belly. What would Father say? And what of the Coombs family? If they hated Indians, what would they think about a *powwaw* living at the near farm?

They would never know. Not unless Grandfather told them himself. And why would he, if his powers had grown weak?

I tried to comfort myself with these thoughts as I brought the hammer and two square nails from the barn. I pounded the nails into the squared log, careful not to bend them.

Grandfather raised his eyebrows. "You like to build things," he said.

'Twas not a question. I studied him. "Do you?" I asked.

"If I need to." Grandfather's mouth twitched into a smile. "What do you wish to make?"

"A canoe." I hadn't planned to tell him, but my secret slipped out. "Would you help me?"

Grandfather didn't answer right away. He hung up a few worn shirts, then placed his own bundles of twigs, roots, and dried herbs on Mother's medicine shelf. I waited. "A canoe takes time," he said at last.

I thought he would say more, but he made up a sleeping pallet, with the wolf skin on top. "I am tired," Grandfather said. He lay down and closed his eyes.

I slipped from the room. *A canoe takes time,* Grandfather had said. And surely he didn't need a canoe. Would he help me? I couldn't puzzle him out.

I stood on our front stoop. My birthday had not started or ended as I planned. My stomach was empty, my brain full of unsettled thoughts, and I'd not seen a single gift.

Mother and Rhoda worked side by side in the garden, gathering the last of the *pompions* and turnips and piling them in baskets. Rhoda's face was half turned toward me. In her nose and her high cheekbones, she favored Grandfather. Like me, Rhoda carried Mother's coloring. Would Hiram tease her, too?

I clenched my fists. Let him try. If Hiram used those ugly names on my sister, I'd show him how a war club worked.

66

11. Daniel

"Daniel." Mother beckoned to me and I went into the garden. She cupped her hand under my chin. "Such fury in your face—what's troubling you?"

"Nothing." I couldn't meet her eyes. "How long will Grandfather stay?"

"As long as he wishes." Mother twisted the stem of a small *pompion* to break it from the vine. The great frost had blackened the vines in the night, and the *pompions,* once hidden beneath the broad leaves, now shone orange against the dark soil. "Help me gather the rest," Mother said.

Rhoda skipped over to us. Her cheeks were red as Mother's russet apples and her breath puffed smoke in the cold. "Maybe Grandfather will stay forever."

"I don't know his plans," Mother said.

"Does Father know?" Rhoda asked.

Father. So much had happened, I'd forgotten I'd run off. What was keeping him? He would be angry with me. I stood still, holding a small *pompion* in my hands. I should have returned to the woodlot with him.

"Daniel, are you in a dream?" Mother handed me the basket of turnips. "Set these on the shelf in the root cellar and close the doors when you're done."

I hauled the basket away without complaint. I held my breath going down the steep ladder and waited a moment, in the dim light, until I could see the shelves, with their neat rows of turnips and potatoes. The cellar smelled damp and musty. I sneezed as I spread the turnips quickly on a shelf. Carrots poked from a barrel of sand, and my stomach growled. Nothing to eat since my porridge this morning— another thing wrong with this day!

I climbed up, closed the heavy doors, and went to the barn, where I fed the sheep and collected eggs from beneath the hens. I even fetched fresh water for the gander, batting him away when he nipped my breeches. Father should be glad if he found the chores done.

Jody yipped and I went outside to see Father striding through shadows as he crossed the meadow ground, then the cornfield. His shoulders slumped under the weight of his tools.

"Go help your father," Mother said. "He looks done in."

Rhoda pushed past me. "Let me tell him," she said.

Fine; let her go first. Perhaps he'd forget my truancy.

Rhoda scrambled over the fence. "Grandfather came! Grandfather is here!" She bounced from one foot to the other.

"Mind the saw." Father set down the bow saw. The ax poked from Mother's basket, nested atop coils of birch bark. He gave me a strange look, then bent to Rhoda. "What did you say?"

"Our grandfather came. He's sleeping inside. Come!" Rhoda yanked on Father's free hand.

Father's eyebrows knitted and he pushed his hat back. "Your grandfather? When?"

"At noontime. He's inside. Hurry!"

Father let Rhoda pull him along. "Bring the tools," he told me. "We will speak later."

So he *was* angered. I followed them down the hill, stowed the tools in the barn, and went to the well when Father asked for fresh water. I brought him a bucketful and tipped it into the basin on the front stoop. We waited while Father washed his face and hands, smoothed his beard, and ran his fingers through his hair, tying it back with rawhide. He looked from Mother to Rhoda and last, to me.

"Well?" he said. "What are we waiting for? Let's go in."

He was afraid. Afraid of Grandfather. Why?

The fire crackled and flames leapt against the stone chimney when we entered the chamber. Grandfather waited at the plank table, his arms crossed over his chest. He wore his deerskin jacket open at the throat. His copper pendant glittered in the firelight. He drew himself up tall.

The two men stared at one another. They made me think on two dogs when they first meet. Father was taller, but he bowed his head as if the traveling parson had come to call. Rhoda tugged on Father's sleeve and broke the silence.

"Say hello to Grandfather," she begged.

Father cleared his throat. "Welcome," he said. "I trust you are comfortable. You have come a long way."

Grandfather nodded. "It was a journey of many days." He gripped the back of the tall bench. "But I had no choice. The others were leaving our village."

"Why?" Mother asked. "Where have they gone?"

Grandfather stood very still. He seemed to watch something behind me. "Many have moved to Indiantown. Now there is talk of starting Christian villages among the Oneida people, far from the *Owamux,* who have taken our land." His eyes grew darker. "English hogs and cattle trample our crops. The English built houses on our hunting grounds. They killed the fish in our streams. Our people work for the *Owamux* as servants, and the old ways are nearly gone."

Grandfather almost spat when he used the Pequot word for the English: *Owamux.* Father rubbed one hand over his eyes. Finally, Mother said, "When the others went away— were you left alone?"

"No. But the village felt empty. I thought of Daniel, and of Rhoda, the granddaughter I had never seen. It was time to find you." He turned to Father. "I rode by your family's farm, where Daniel was born. Strangers live there, since your parents died."

"Yes," Father said. "I know."

My grandfather's eyes seemed to sink deep into his skull. Shadows filled the front chamber. We all stared at the empty spaces in the corners. Rhoda grabbed Mother's skirt and wound herself in the wool folds. I jumped when a log popped, sending sparks onto the hearth. Father's hand was heavy on my shoulder. "Help me finish the chores," he said.

"I fed the animals," I said, but Father beckoned and I shrugged into my wool jacket. Time for my punishment.

I followed him through the shed that held the privy and on into the barn. Father sat on the sill of the open barn door. "Sit down with me," he said. I found a place beside him. The sun had fallen behind the mountains. The animals chewed and rustled their bedding. My thoughts were not as peaceful as the evening settling over us.

"I'm sorry for what you heard this afternoon," Father said. He set a hand on my knee. "I knew the boy was lying."

"How?"

"You're the only one skilled enough to catch that fish with your bare hands. When I saw what they'd done, I nearly followed you home myself."

A smile loosened my chest. "In truth?"

"Aye. I only stayed because they're in a bad way, moving here with winter coming on."

"Mrs. Coombs doesn't like me," I said.

"I'm not sure she likes anyone," Father said. "She's mean-spirited. Coombs won't say a word against her, though perhaps he means well. If he hadn't promised to help us finish our harvest, I'd have left him high and dry." He shook his head. "Foolish woman. She'll need a doctress like your mother when her time comes, but she won't hear of it."

"Is she having a baby?" I asked.

"Yes. She's in for a hard time of it, starting out here so late in the season—but it's hard to pity such an ill-tempered woman."

Our eyes met in the dusk. "Don't let that boy bother you," Father said. "He learned his bad ways from his family. You have nothing to be ashamed of." He cleared his throat. "And please, keep this from your mother."

"I will." It warmed me inside, to share a secret with Father, even a secret with such a sharp edge. For the first time all day, I felt grown, as if being thirteen had changed things. "But, Father——"

"Yes."

"Must we go back tomorrow?"

"No." Father chuckled. "Too much to do here." He mussed my hair. I hugged myself. No punishment! Even better, no Hiram on the morrow—perhaps never.

We were quiet a moment. The first star pricked the sky. "Father, are you *Owamux?* English?"

He tugged his beard. "Your grandfather speaks that word like an oath, doesn't he? I was born in England, but I supported the Patriot cause, though I only mustered out with our local militia."

"That's why you had to fight, in the raid."

"Yes," Father said. "But now the war is ended, we are all Americans. They say Vermont may even join the Union soon." He stood up and closed the barn door, sliding the bar across. "The chores are finished?"

"Yes, except for the milking."

"All right. Go inside and get warm. And, son? We won't mention Mrs. Coombs to Rhoda, either. She's too young to understand."

"All right." Although the cold had seeped through my coat, I stood near the sheep pen, puzzling on Father's words. If Father was *Owamux,* and Mother a Pequot—then who was I?

Part II

Stranger from the North

12. Hiram

Smoke come out the chimbley for the first time when I got home. Pa was chopping wood in the foreyard.

"Pa!" I cried. I set down the buckets. "Pa—there's an Injun chief next door!"

He set down the ax. I come close and seen his cheeks was smudged and his eyes tired.

"There's a chief, with arrows and a tomahawk and all. He's just like them Injuns what carried Uncle Abner away!"

"Hiram, I've about had enough," Pa said. "First you run off, shaming me in front of the new neighbors. I'm certain you stole that fish. Then you leave your ma here alone—"

"She was sleeping!" We was both talking low now, so she wouldn't hear us. "I went to get more water, that's all."

"Sounds like you've been spying on the neighbors," Pa said.

"But there's Injuns, Pa. I seen them."

"Hiram, listen to me," Pa said. "Mr. Tucker is married to a Pequot Indian woman. You heard him yourself. That's his business, not yours or mine."

"But, Pa—"

He held up his hand. The look in his eye meant trouble. "Fetch the water inside for your ma," Pa told me. "She's working too hard, which is more than I can say for you." He leaned close and I smelled cider on his breath. "No stories, you hear? Your ma has enough to worry about." He shooed me away.

Stories. So that's what Pa thought. All right. I'd keep my mouth shut. If Pa wanted to get scalped by some Injun chief, let him.

Ma kept me running till supper. Just this morning, she'd cried about that big stump in the middle of the room. Not tonight. She set supper on the stump like it was our best table board. But what she put on it weren't much—just some apples left over from the Tuckers' basket and some suppawn. Porridge don't taste good without milk, but I durst not complain.

It was near dark inside. Pa set a pitch pine knot on the hearth to burn. Ma was saving our Betty lamp in case we had company. Shadows shifted in the corners and made me jumpy. Finally, Ma said, "Hiram—stop that fidgeting. What's eating you?"

I was about to tell her the truth, spite of Pa's warning, when someone shouted outside. I jumped up and grabbed Ma's arm. "Ma, hide!"

Ma stared at me. "Have you lost your senses?" she asked, and pushed past me. We went to the door and peered out. Two men stood where our path meets the road, holding up a torch. We couldn't see who they were with the sun near gone.

"Halloo!" one of them called. "Mr. Coombs?"

"Isaac, who is it?" Ma whispered. "We can't have company now. Our house ain't fit for swine."

"Coombs, here," Pa shouted. "Can I help you?"

"It's Durkee, the miller," the tall man called out. "Someone's here to see you."

"Durkee's the man who give us directions this morning," Pa said. He waved to the men. "Come on up!"

We waited while they zigzagged up the hill. The other man leaned on Mr. Durkee, dragging his leg like he had a big stone attached to his foot.

"One of them's hurt," I said.

Just then, Jed starts to bellow. *"Moo-ah! Moo-ah!"*

"What's got into the ox?" Pa asked.

"God save us," Ma said, and took off. Heavy as she was, Ma run to the men and throwed her arms around the one with the limp. He staggered and near fell down.

Pa and I hurried after. I didn't understand a thing, even when Ma cried, "Abner! Abner! We thought you'd been murdered!"

Uncle Abner? I nearly keeled over myself. I stared at him while Ma clutched the man tight and Pa clapped his shoulder.

I hung back. Even with Mr. Durkee's torchlight on his face, I knew this weren't my uncle. Couldn't be. Why, Uncle Abner was husky, with a red beard and strong arms. *This* man was skin and bones, with his clothes in rags. My uncle held himself straight, but this man was hunched over, his shoulders caved in around his chest. But when Ma let go and Pa pumped the man's hand up and down like a well handle, I seen his smile with that missing tooth. Could it be?

"Hiram?" He hobbled over to me. "This can't be my nephew. You got too big." He set his hand on my shoulder and set me to jiggling, he was shivering so hard.

"Uncle Abner." My voice come out in a squeak. "I knew you'd come back. You weren't scalped, were you?" I tried to see my uncle's hair under his hat.

"Hush," Ma said.

Abner took off his hat and showed us his hair, all greasy and matted in the torchlight. "Still got my hair," he said. "I was one of the lucky ones."

"Excuse me." The miller cleared his throat. We'd plumb forgot he was there. "I'd better go along," Mr. Durkee said. He raised his torch so he lit our faces and I saw that Pa—my own pa!—had wet cheeks.

"We're much obliged to you," Pa said. "How'd he find you?"

"I was headed to Royalton, to find our old place—" Uncle Abner said, but then he started in coughing.

"He's tuckered out," Mr. Durkee said. "Take him inside and get him warm. Let me know if I can help. We had a good harvest this year and I can spare some grain. If it's doctoring you need, you're in luck. Miz Tucker's right next door."

Ma give Pa a funny look but didn't say nothing. Pa and Uncle Abner thanked Mr. Durkee again, and then we helped my uncle inside.

Seems as if Uncle Abner was just holding himself together until he found us, because it took all three of us to get him up over the one step and through the door. "Set him in the rocker," Pa said. "That bench is no good for him, without a back on it."

Ma wiped her face and began fussing over Uncle Abner like he was the new baby. She lit the Betty lamp and sent Pa and me to pour warm water from the iron kettle into a basin she set on the dirt by his feet. I couldn't hardly believe what I saw. My uncle didn't have any shoes. His feet was wrapped in rags, and when Ma untied the wrappings, there was a sour smell of dried blood and worse. Uncle Abner groaned.

We give my uncle apples and the rest of the suppawn, but he didn't want much. "Mr. Durkee fed me a bit," Uncle Abner said. "He told me not to eat too fast. We lived on bark and strips of meat from a heifer we killed when we were on the run. My stomach's small as a banty hen's egg." He begun to cough again, and I patted his back.

Pa give him a wooden noggin of cider to sip on. Uncle Abner held it like it was a precious cone of real sugar while we wrapped him in a blanket.

"I thank you," he said to Ma. He looked at me, then at Pa. Was it the shadows cast by the Betty lamp that made his eyes so strange? They was set awful deep in his head.

"What did those Injuns do to you?" I asked.

"Hiram!" Ma cried.

"I'm sorry," I said. I wanted to hide, but there was no place to go. My tough uncle Abner—the one who taught me to cuss when Ma wasn't listening, who showed me how to skin a rabbit and make a slingshot, who learnt me to whistle through my teeth—this same brave uncle begun to cry. His hands shook so hard Pa took the mug away.

"Hiram, shame on you." Pa gave me a look that shriveled me up. I might have been a leech sprinkled with salt.

Uncle Abner shook his head. "Don't blame the boy." He stared at his feet in the basin, then wiped his eyes. "Those Injuns were bad. They murdered some men, burned houses, killed our cattle. But the Redcoats was worse than the savages." He give Ma a long, sad look. "That's why we escaped. Dug ourselves outta that prison like blind moles. And now, after all that, we hear the war's finished and the rest of the prisoners is free men. Be just my luck if they beat me home—"

He liked to have a fit with his coughing. Ma patted him on the back, and Pa held the noggin of cider up to his cracked lips. When he caught his breath he said, "It's not for young ears. And not a story for tonight."

No one said a word. Questions bubbled up hard in my throat, but I swallowed them down. How could the Redcoats be worse than the Injuns?

My uncle begun to shake again and Pa stoked up the fire. "Twenty-two days sleeping on the ground," Uncle Abner said. "I believe what I need most is a bed."

I glanced at Ma and she nodded. "Ma and I made a hemlock bed today," I told him. "You can sleep there."

Before long, we had Uncle Abner settled on the only soft pallet in the place. I rolled myself in a blanket near the fire, but I couldn't sleep, no more than Ma or Pa could. Ma set in her chair with her hands on her belly. Pa lay out on that stump, staring into the fire. I knew we was all wondering the same thing: What had they done to my uncle?

13. Daniel

Mother was filling our trenchers with a mix of corn and beans when Father and I came back from the barn. *"Sooktash!"* Grandfather said.

We washed it down with cider while Mother laughed and chattered, asking Grandfather a thousand questions. She and Grandfather switched back and forth from Pequot to English. I tried to follow, but they spoke too fast. Mother seemed to ask about friends and relatives she'd left behind in Connecticut. I couldn't always puzzle out Grandfather's answers. Sometimes he didn't speak but stared into the fire. That's when I guessed that someone had died, or moved away.

When I scraped my bowl clean, Father set a hand on my knee. "Could you check your grandfather's mare again? Give her some extra hay—she's had a long journey."

Would my birthday never end? Still not a single gift. My

eyes stung and I was pleased no one saw my face as I slipped through the shed and into the barn. The sweet smell of hay took my mind back to summer, when the neighbors came to help Father rake the hay into windrows, then stack it into haycocks. It was peaceful then. No Hiram, nor Grandfather, either. What if neither one had come to our hillside?

I forked hay into the manger for the mare and straightened her mane, combing out the tangles. "You're a fine old horse," I whispered. "Take no heed of my silly thoughts. Father and I will care for you, just like the other animals in our barn. And of course I'm glad Grandfather is here."

The mare whickered. I touched her muzzle, soft as worn buckskin, and took myself inside. The house smelled of maple sugar. My stomach spoke to me, even though I'd cleaned my trencher. When I sat to unbutton my coat, Rhoda clapped her hands across my eyes.

"Surprise!" she cried.

I twisted away. Rhoda stood betwixt me and the table, holding out her arms to block the view.

"Don't look," she said.

At last! I couldn't keep back a smile. "Let me see." I poked her at the waist.

She skipped to the table. "*Now* look," she said.

A wampum belt lay on the table board. White and purple shells made a pattern like the step design on one of Mother's prize baskets. I looked to Mother, then Grandfather, who stood in front of the fire. "This is for me?"

Grandfather nodded. I lifted the belt carefully and held it across the front of my breeches; tied the soft leather straps behind my waist.

"The belt belonged to my father's father," Grandfather said. "It has been passed from grandfather to grandson. You are old enough to care for it now. When a man carries a belt with such *mundtu,* he possesses wealth and power. The Dutch and the English once traded in wampum. A messenger could also carry a wampum belt as a message to another tribe." His eyes held mine, as Jody holds the sheep when she corners them. "If you were a *powwaw,* it would be fitting for you to wear."

Powwaw. That word again. My throat went dry. I set the belt down on the table. If I put it on, did this mean I had agreed to become a *powwaw?* Mother had told me how, in the past, Pequot boys my age would go out into the woods for three, four, even five nights, fasting and waiting for a vision or dream to speak to them. Grandfather might expect this of me, but not Father. Could I refuse?

Mother cleared her throat and nodded at me. "Thank you, Grandfather," I said quickly. *"Tabut ne."* Still, I stepped away, in case the belt held magic.

Mother stood before me with her hands behind her back, her eyes twinkling. "Which hand?" she asked.

"Right," I said, pointing. She shook her head. "Mother, don't tease." We had played this game since I was younger than Rhoda. We both laughed as I gripped her left arm and pried her fingers open to find a soft deerskin pouch. A rawhide string tied the pouch closed at the top, and criss-crossed quill beading decorated the bottom.

Rhoda clapped her hands. "You can hang it on your new belt!"

"Thank you, Mother," I said. "When did you make it?"

"At night," she said. "When you slept."

I stroked the silky deerskin. Mother must have spent long hours softening the hide, collecting the quills, then weaving them into this beautiful pattern.

The front door closed and Father came in with an armload of wood. He built up the fire, brushed bark from his coat, and studied the wampum belt. "Whose is this?" he asked.

"Mine now," I told him. "A gift from Grandfather."

Father held the belt to the firelight. "These quahog shells were once worth a lot of money. Too bad you can't use the belt for currency now. It might buy more than our worthless Continental bills."

Rhoda wiggled her stool closer to the table. "Grandfather says the belt will make Daniel into a *powwaw*."

Father's gray eyes narrowed. "Don't be foolish," he said. "Daniel is still a boy. And a belt can't turn Daniel into someone else. Besides, we don't have *powwaws* now, do we?" He looked at Grandfather.

"Caleb." Mother took hold of Father's wrists and pulled him around so he was looking into her face. "Where would you be now, if my father had *not* been a *powwaw?*"

"What do you mean?" Rhoda asked.

"'Tis true. I misspoke." Father sank onto the high-backed bench. His shoulders drooped and he looked ashamed. "Your mother and her father saved my life when I nearly drowned."

"How?" Rhoda asked.

"You know that story," Father said.

Rhoda tugged his sleeve. "Tell it again," she begged.

"All right." Father pulled her onto his lap. "I was half dead when Mother's family pulled me from the river," he said. "They pushed the water from my belly, dressed my wound, kept me warm and safe until I could walk again." He touched his forehead. "And then Kate said she'd marry me, in spite of my ugly scar." He held his hands out toward Grandfather. "Forgive me. I wasn't thinking."

Grandfather nodded. The silence in the room felt too big. I took up my new pouch and handed it to Father. "Look what Mother gave me."

Father turned the pouch over, then opened it and looked inside. "So this is what you were making the last few nights." He smiled at her. "'Tis not for tobacco, is it?"

Mother shook her head. "Of course not. Daniel can keep his treasures in it." She took Father's arm. "Did *you* forget to bring a gift?"

Father slapped his forehead as if he *had* forgotten, but I knew he meant to tease me. He lifted Rhoda from his lap and pretended to search his pockets. "Now, where is that—

I'm sure it's here somewhere—" He dug into his coat. "Ah—here it is!" Father pulled out a leather sheath holding a knife. "Happy birthday, son."

"Oh." My fingers shook. I tugged at the bone handle. Smooth and cool beneath my fingers. The curved blade winked in the firelight. A man's knife. As big as Father's. The knife spoke of danger and of beauty. "Thank you, Father." I could barely speak. Father knew me better than I'd thought. 'Twas the perfect present.

"A fine gift," Grandfather said. He bent over the wood box and gave me a small length of pine. "Here. See how it cuts."

I sat beside the fire and sliced the blade along the grain of the wood. The knife made a deep cut into the pine. Thin slivers curled onto the stone hearth.

Rhoda perched on the high-backed bench, watching with wide eyes. "Will you make me something?" she asked.

"Of course," I said. "What would you like?"

"A doll."

How to fashion a doll from a block of pine? That might be hard. But how soothing, to push the blade through the wood, to feel the knife's power. Would Hiram have such a knife? No. Mr. Coombs said he couldn't trust Hiram with the ax—yet Father believed I was old enough for a knife.

Mother opened the oven door, slipped the long-handled slice under the *pompion,* and set it on the table board. Steam poured from the hole at the top. The syrup's sweet smell tickled my nose. I remembered the muddy spring days when we gathered maple sap and boiled it outside in the iron kettle. The *pompion's* skin was pleated and soft.

"It's my big *pompion!*" Rhoda cried. "Mother cooked it all day."

"Daniel, would you carve it with your knife?" Mother asked.

I held the knife above the *pompion* for a second, then plunged the blade through the skin, following the curving line that nature had drawn for me. A second cut and the *pompion* fell open. Steaming milk, laced with syrup, spilled out of the *pompion* into the dish. I cut while Mother set each piece in a wooden bowl, spooning the hot, sweet milk over the top. I blew on the first bite to cool it. "Thank you, Mother."

My bowl clean, my belly full to bursting, I stood to clear my place. "Look, Caleb." Mother pulled me close, set a hand atop my head. "He nearly reaches my shoulder. Soon he will be taller than you are."

"He will grow a little more, then stop," Grandfather said in a firm voice.

I stared. Grandfather's voice was a warning.

"How can you know my son's future?" Father's scar pulsed in the candlelight. "Let the boy alone." He walked away without another word, ducking behind the curtains drawn around his and Mother's bed. Jody trotted after him with her tail between her legs.

The chamber was warm from the fire, but still I shivered. 'Twas not like Father to speak so sharply. Grandfather's eyes were like the coals glowing on the hearth. He pulled his deerskin jacket close over his chest, said good night, and disappeared as well, his moccasins whispering on the puncheon floor.

Rhoda and I cleaned our bowls. Mother took up her basket and began twisting her strips of ash. As if the day had never happened, as if 'twere morning all over again. I felt like those strips of wood, yanked and tugged in every direction.

Rhoda leaned against me. "Will we see the yellow-haired boy tomorrow?"

"I hope not." I bit my lip, remembering Father's warning.

"'Twas cruel to laugh at him," Mother said. "You must take him a gift."

A gift? For Hiram? Never. I laid the wampum belt on the mantel. Rhoda grabbed my hand and pulled me toward the loft. "Let's play hubbub," she said.

I didn't want to play at anything, but I followed her up the ladder to our pallets.

"Did you like my present?" Rhoda asked.

I peered at my sister. A frown tugged at the corners of her mouth. "The *pompion* was my favorite present," I said, although in truth the knife pleased me more. "'Twas delicious." I searched beneath the eaves for the wooden hubbub bowl with its black and white chips and shook it hard. Two white pieces flipped out.

"Don't!" Rhoda said. "You'll lose them." She scrambled for the pieces and returned them to the bowl. I let her shake for the second round, then the third. It mattered not whether the pieces came up white or black; I let Rhoda be first to call "Hubbub!"

"Please play," Rhoda said.

I crawled beneath my blankets, still dressed, and closed my eyes against the firelight washing up and down the rafters. If I slept, this birthday would be gone. Gone until next year, when the geese flew south again.

14. Daniel

I woke to silence and daylight. In the front chamber, I found cold jonnycake laid out on the table beside my knife.

I slipped the knife from its sheath. Sunlight caught the blade. Metal cold and dangerous beneath my fingertips. "*Wegun,*" I whispered. "So good. You are a good knife."

The knife sat, waiting, as I gobbled my food. I settled it back in its pouch, strapped it to my belt, hugged it to my hip. Already a good friend.

"When Gander Head sees you, he will fear me." But what was I saying? I hoped never to see Hiram again.

My new deerskin pouch lay on the bench. I rubbed it against my cheek to feel its smooth softness, then hooked it on the other side of my belt and went outside. A bitter smell tickled my nostrils. Smoke lay across the hills like a blanket, a sign the neighbors were making potash for the Boston market.

Grandfather stood atop the hill among the wheat stubble,

working over his mare. He buckled the harness under her belly. Father's sledge stood beside them. Where was he going?

I started for the fence when the gander honked behind me. *"Whee! Honkity-wronk wronk!"*

A woman's voice hailed me. "Anyone home?"

I squinted. Mrs. Ellis, from the near farm, stood at the gate. I took up a stick and ran to head off the gander, swatting at its tail.

"Thank you, Daniel." Mrs. Ellis came through the gate, her frame almost too wide for the opening. She pointed to her cheek, swollen like a chipmunk's after nut gathering. "Is your mother in? I've a terrible toothache."

Rhoda ran up to us, out of breath. "She's in the kitchen garden. Wintergreen is fine for a toothache."

"Aren't you smart." Mrs. Ellis peered at Rhoda. "You'll be a fine Indian doctress someday, like your mother. As good as that Molly Ockutt folks talk about."

"Thank you, ma'am." Rhoda's smile showed the gap where her front teeth were missing.

"Shall I take you to Mother?" I asked.

Mrs. Ellis pushed her bonnet back and peered at the wheat field through her round spectacles. "You have company?"

"Grandfather is here," I said.

"My goodness!" Mrs. Ellis's laugh rang false. "Kate's father?"

I nodded. "He came last night."

"What a surprise!" She rubbed her swollen cheek. "I hope there won't be trouble, with the prisoners just released."

"What prisoners?" I asked.

She pursed her lips. "Never mind. I misspoke." She turned her back on us. "Go along, I'll find Kate myself. What news, what news!"

Rhoda took my hand. "Why will we have trouble?"

"I don't know. Come on, let's see what Grandfather is doing." I whistled to Jody. We climbed the fence and hurried across the meadow ground. From a distance, Grandfather might have been any of the neighbors, in his flannel shirt and heavy breeches, but the gray braid that fell to his waist marked him as a Pequot. As I came close, I spied Father's tools on the sledge: felling ax, bucksaw, bark spud. Rhoda ran on ahead of me.

"Where are you going?" Rhoda asked.

"Into the forest." Grandfather wiggled the bit against the mare's teeth, then slipped it into her mouth when her jaw opened, and drew the bridle over her ears. He stroked her neck. "Today we will build a wigwam."

We? "Why?" I asked.

"I need my own home," Grandfather said.

"Why don't you live with us?" Rhoda asked.

"It's better this way." Grandfather hitched the traces to the sledge.

Had Father's words last night driven him out? Was this a good thing? I felt uneasy, as if a summer storm rumbled on the far side of our river valley.

"Where will you build it?" I asked.

"Near the oak." He pointed to the knoll, where the black oak stood alone, a sentinel guarding the wheat field.

"How do you make a wigwam?" I asked.

"I will teach you. It's time for you to learn the old ways."

My throat went dry. *Was* it time? Father didn't think so. "I know some of those ways," I told him. "Mother taught me to build a fish weir, and I caught a big trout there, with my own hands. I can name animals by their tracks and other signs. I can find the four directions, and walk through the forest without making a sound."

"That is a good beginning," Grandfather said.

"I'm learning, too," Rhoda said.

"Yes," Grandfather said. "But you must wait."

Rhoda's mouth turned down. I took her hand. "Mother is already teaching Rhoda about her medicines," I told Grandfather, "even though she is young. Mrs. Ellis, our neighbor, just said that Rhoda will be a fine doctress someday."

"Wegun," Grandfather said. "Good. But this is a job for men. We use sharp, heavy tools." He touched Rhoda's head. "Later, when we cut cedar saplings for the frame, you can help us strip the bark."

"All right," Rhoda said. She squared her shoulders, as if to make herself look older. "I'll show you to the cedar grove when you come back."

"Take Jody, so you won't be lonesome," I said. I watched Rhoda trudge down the hill. Jody loped beside her. My sister was brave, yet she looked forlorn now, like a lost bird.

I felt Grandfather's eyes on me. "Where are we going?" I asked.

"To the neighbors." Grandfather pointed to the forest.

"Your father told me to cut bark from the trees you felled yesterday. You can lead me there."

My feet stayed fastened to the wheat stubble. "You're taking wood from Mr. Coombs?"

"Only the bark," Grandfather said. "Come along."

Worries flew in and out of my brain. I thought of Hiram's mother, regarding me with eyes of stone, and of his father's uneasiness when first he spied my dark skin. What would the Coombses say about Grandfather?

"Where is Father?" I asked.

"At a barn raising." He clucked to the mare and she leaned into the traces.

I nearly turned around. Father went to raisings only because he had to, but I liked to watch the men hoist the timbers with ropes and pulleys. Now that I had my knife, I could whittle trunnels and give them to the men when they were ready to peg the beams. Of course, Grandfather was building something, too, so why did I drag my feet?

Because of Gander Head, of course.

The sledge bumped over the rutted ground and I hurried after the old man. He was a *powwaw* with special powers. He could take care of himself, and he'd protect me—wouldn't he?

I touched my knife before I caught up to Grandfather and followed the sledge into the timber.

15. Hiram

When Pa heard chopping up in the forest, he asked me to see if Mr. Tucker come back. "Tell him we have to finish the chimbley," Pa said. "Maybe we can lumber again tomorrow."

I laced my boots. I was happy to escape from Ma and Uncle Abner. She was fussing over him, trying to soothe that cough that kept us awake all night. Every time I got near and asked about his capture, she shooed me away.

Atop the hill, I heard chopping and sawing, then voices. Who was it? I ducked behind a white pine with a trunk tall as a ship's mast and gasped. Injuns again! Daniel was there with the chief—but the old man didn't look much like a chief today. He had on clothes like Pa's. A bony horse stood hitched to a sledge. It had a swayback worse than Ma's, and its head near dragged on the ground.

Hold on—they was stealing Pa's wood! I crawled closer and hid behind an oak. The old man sawed up a tree like it came from his own forest. I was about to holler when I seen something funny. The old man pried the bark off the tree, making a big slab long as my arm. Daniel throwed the slab onto the sledge, but they left the good fire log laying on the ground. I tried not to laugh. Who ever heard of taking the bark and leaving the tree?

I edged closer, but a stick snapped under me just when things were quiet. I dove into the brush. The old man reached into his pouch and something rattled in the leaves. Stones rained down on my head!

"Ouch!" I yelped. "Quit!" I scrambled to my feet. That old man held a slingshot. It was acorns falling on me, not stones, but they still stung. I started to run.

"Yellow Hair! Stop!" the chief yelled.

Now, that made me so mad I whirled around. "You stop," I said. "My name ain't Yellow Hair. I don't call you Gray Hair, do I?"

I swear, the old man's laugh sounded like a cow when it's got the heaves, but I wouldn't laugh with him. "You're thieves!" I yelled. "Stealing Pa's wood."

"You're the thief," Daniel said, "stealing my fish."

The chief hushed him with his strange words and waved me over. I took a few steps but didn't come too close. Daniel had a knife on his belt with a smooth handle. The sheath looked brand-new. I wished I had one like that, but of course I didn't say nothing.

"Daniel and his father helped with the cutting, so your father offered us some of this wood," the old man said. "We only take the bark. It's of no use to you."

"Bark makes a bad fire," I told him.

"Yes," the old man said. "But a good wigwam."

"Wigwam? What's that?"

The boy Daniel shook his head, like I was stupid.

"A wigwam is a Pequot home," the chief said. And then, before I knew what was happening, he picked up one of them bark slabs, set it in my arms, and pointed me to the sledge. "The work goes faster with three," he said.

My knees almost buckled under the bark. "I don't have to help you," I told him.

"No," the chief said. He pointed at my hands. "Such smooth palms. Perhaps you are not used to hard work?"

Daniel snorted and that decided me. I wouldn't let them think I was no weakling. Besides, Uncle Abner would want to know if they was building an Injun house next door. So I stumbled to the sledge and dumped the bark, then picked up another slab, heavier than the first one.

I kept quiet, listening to their talk. First, the old man said things in his language; then they switched to English—but they still didn't talk like people I'm used to. The chief sounded like he'd swallowed gravel, and Daniel's voice reminded me of something. What was it?

The old man's tool fell over near my feet. When I didn't move, Daniel said, "Hand it to me."

I didn't move. "You talk like a Tory," I said. I didn't tell him he sounded like that Redcoat lieutenant in the raid. "I bet you was with the Loyalists, in the war."

"Never," Daniel said. He puffed out his chest. "We're Patriots. Grandfather, too."

Now who was lying? An Injun can't be a Patriot. Any fool knows that.

"Daniel. Bring the bark spud," the old man said. Daniel sent me a nasty look, then held the log so it wouldn't tip over while his grandpa used the spud to pry off the bark. He grunted like a swine trying to pry it loose. "Spring is a better time to build a wigwam," the grandpa said. "The bark falls away easier then."

I kept on hauling the slabs. My hands blistered, but I didn't let on. "How do you make these into a house?" I asked.

"If you come to Daniel's tomorrow, we will show you," the old man said.

Daniel's face got dark and he whispered some words at the old man in that other language.

"Don't worry," I told them. "I ain't coming to see no dirty Injun place."

"Stop that!" Daniel lunged at me. I made fists, but the old man stuck his arm between us and pushed Daniel away. The chief grabbed my shirt so hard I thought he'd tear it.

"You must not use that word," the chief said. "Ever."

"What word? Let go a me!" I pushed him and kicked his shins. "He shouldn't call me names, either!"

The old man gripped my shoulders and time went backwards two years, right downriver to Royalton. The neighbor who got scalped stared at me with dead eyes. I saw the Injun's face full of murder as he hauled me away. The spear stuck out a Uncle Abner's leg. Dead oxen littered the road. Was that me screaming, or the woman who lost her husband?

I tore outta there, jumping logs and branches, and fell down in the dry leaves, bawling. Good thing I was alone. When my breath come back, I rolled over and let the sun dry my face. Then Ma's voice rose in the distance. I sat up.

No one behind me. No Injuns. Nothing but branches waving in the wind.

I lay there awhile until I got a chill. I must be a lunatic. Why else would I hear those sounds?

16. Daniel

"Yellow Hair hates us," I told Grandfather.

"No. He is afraid. A demon lives inside him." Grandfather sighed. "It is a bad disease."

"Yellow Hair isn't sick," I told Grandfather. "He has no sense, and he's full of malice."

"He has an ailment you can't see," Grandfather said. "Perhaps you will understand later."

"An *Owamux* disease?" I asked.

He grunted. Was that an answer?

I gathered my courage. "Grandfather," I said, "if I had the canker rash, or some disease—could you cure me? I'm half *Owamux*. And so is Rhoda."

Grandfather's eyes darkened and I felt ashamed of my rudeness. "A foolish question," he said. "You are healthy." He took up the bark spud again.

My words came before I could think on them. "But, Grandfather—if you cannot cure the diseases of the *Owamux*—and since I am half *Owamux*—how could I become a *powwaw?* I would only have half your power. No, not half—even less."

Grandfather flinched as if he'd bit on a stone in his food. "Enough of this talk." His voice was sharp.

My stomach twisted, but not from any relish for food. I had caught him out, but I took no pleasure in making him angry. I hauled the final slabs to the sledge and balanced them on the pile.

The sun licked the maple leaves with orange and yellow flames. We set off for home in silence. The mare leaned into the harness as the sledge bumped and lurched over the rough ground. Grandfather walked on one side of the pile while I held the other. Together, we kept the slabs from sliding off.

We unhitched the mare near the lone oak and left the slabs and the sledge beneath the tree. Still we didn't speak. Jody barked and Rhoda came running. Her braids whipped from side to side and I felt relieved to see her.

"Daniel! Grandfather!" she hailed us in her high voice. "We cut the cedar poles. Mother and I did it together. Can we build the wigwam now?"

"Not yet," Grandfather said. "But soon."

The mare whinnied at Rhoda. "The mare likes you," I told her.

Rhoda smiled and caught my hand. Her breath came fast. "What's her name?" she asked.

Grandfather spoke a long Pequot word we didn't understand.

"Can I give her an English name?" Rhoda asked.

"If you like," Grandfather said.

"Thank you." Rhoda led the mare across the mowing ground and up to the foreyard. She stood on tiptoe to stroke the mare's ears. "Look," Rhoda said. "Her ears are pink inside. Like a rabbit's." She laughed. "I will call her Rabbit."

Grandfather glanced at me. Was that a wink?

I smiled and took the mare's bridle. "All right, Rabbit," I said. "Time for hay and water." We led the horse to the barn and rubbed her down.

After we fed her, Rhoda found Grandfather near the sledge and tugged on his sleeve. "Look at our pile of saplings," she said. "Did we cut enough?"

Grandfather nodded, then patted her head. "Your mother remembers the wigwam she grew up in. It looks just right."

Rhoda's square face widened with her smile. *Wegun,* I thought. Grandfather had a kind answer at last.

We stripped bark from the cedar saplings until near candle-lighting time. I was glad for my knife. I slid its sharp point under the bark to free it; then Rhoda took the end and peeled it back. Tangled ribbons of bark fell to the ground, leaving the cedar poles bare and spindly as the arms of Yellow Hair.

I crawled into my pallet soon after supper. My shoulders ached, and a splinter stung my palm, but I was too tired to ask Mother's help in pulling it. Voices stitched in and out of my dreams.

Blankets covered Rhoda's head at first light. I smelled smoke, though the loft was cold. The sound of my belly bump on the ladder woke my sister. She whispered my name.

"Go back to sleep," I told her.

Silence.

In the front chamber, a cold hearth. I opened the door and went out in my nightshirt. Grandfather stood at our sugaring kettle, stoking a fire. The gander honked as Mother whistled to me from the gate. Jack Frost had come to bite the grass again, so I danced over his icy blades, running to Mother.

She sat astride the mare, carrying her medicine basket. "Open the gate," she said, and looked at my feet. "Where are your moccasins? One pegged-out child is enough for today."

Mother's voice was worn and her skin seemed tight across her cheekbones. I led the horse up to the foreyard. "Who's ill?"

"Mrs. Ellis's niece." Mother slid from the mare's back. "Tie up the horse. You can feed her once you are dressed." Her eyes found Grandfather. "Father, what are you doing?" she called.

Grandfather pointed to the saplings, then to the steaming kettle.

"He's going to soak them?" I asked Mother. "Why?"

"So that he can bend them for the frame of the wigwam. Just as I do with my ash splints. Go on," Mother said, "you're shivering. Find your clothes."

The door opened. Rhoda stood on the sill, half dressed. Her braids were tangled, her cheek wrinkled with sleep. "What was the sickness?" Rhoda asked.

Mother didn't answer but walked to the house with slow steps. Rhoda and I followed her inside. I climbed into the loft, but their voices drifted up to me as I dressed. "Mrs. Ellis's niece is poorly," Mother said. "I gave her willow bark tea. Can you guess what was ailing her?"

"A fever?" Rhoda said.

"*Wegun*. Another fine doctress," Mother said. "You are learning fast."

Though I could not see her face, I knew Rhoda would be glad. She liked to know who was ill and how to cure their sickness. I pulled my breeches on, ducking my head under the rafters, then stilled myself. Every day, Rhoda studied Mother's medicines and helped her gather healing roots, bark, and plants. Could Rhoda, my own sister, be a *powwaw*? Hadn't she felt the hawk's *mundtu* and told us someone was coming? Perhaps she had visions already. I had none. I would ask Grandfather about this while we built the wigwam, although he might not answer me.

But the day didn't come about as I'd planned. When I went outside, I found Father and Grandfather arguing on either side of the split-rail fence. Father's arms were crossed over his chest and his bearded chin was pointed at the old man, while Grandfather stood with his legs planted like two trees, clutching a bundle of twine. What was wrong?

Father caught sight of me before I could slip away, and he beckoned me over. "We're having a difference of opinion," Father said, though I didn't care to know about their argument. "Your grandfather wants your help with the wigwam, but I can't spare you this morning. Mr. Shaw sends his freight wagons to Boston. We need to load up our goods and deliver them. Jemmy and Old Red are ready." Father pointed to the barn door, where our oxen stood, yoked and waiting.

I shifted from foot to foot. I couldn't read Grandfather's thoughts under his hooded eyes. "Could I load the goods and then stay to build the wigwam?"

"Not this time," Father said. "You can help when we come home."

"I'm sorry, Grandfather," I said.

Grandfather's eyes stayed on Father. "Your son must learn the old ways as well as the new," he said.

"Perhaps," Father said. "There is plenty of time for learning."

Grandfather cupped his ear and tipped his head to the side, as if listening to something in the distance. I heard nothing but the hens, muttering in the foreyard.

"You can't know how much time we have," Grandfather said.

I shivered and looked up. The sky was clear, but I thought I'd felt a cloud cover the sun. What did Grandfather mean?

Father pushed back his hat and looked Grandfather straight in the eyes. "His place is with me today."

Grandfather turned his back and I slipped away to the barn.

We loaded the wagon with goods Mr. Shaw would sell in

Boston. Grandfather kept to himself while the rest of us stowed a barrel of apples, two sacks of wheat, and a bushel of turnips in the wagon buck. Mother set her finished basket atop the pile, filled with cones of maple sugar from last spring's boiling.

"Not a big load," Father said, "but it will help us buy tea and calico, and perhaps even bring in a few shillings." He touched the gap between Rhoda's sleeve and her wrist. "You grew like your *pompion* vines this summer. You'll need a new dress for winter."

Rhoda hugged herself. "Can I have red calico this time? Please? Or a new pelisse, instead of my old coat?"

"*May* I," Father said, correcting her. "We'll see what purchases Shaw will make. Perhaps we'll use the coins to buy the wool shirting Mrs. Ellis makes on her loom."

"Oh no!" I clutched my belly. "'Tis like wearing nettles."

"Not wool shirting!" Rhoda jumped and twitched, as if she'd stepped in a wasp's nest. "It makes you itch all over!"

Father and Mother laughed. "All right," Father said. "We'll try not to put you in misery." He picked up his willow switch and clucked to the team. "Come along, boys. You, too, Daniel."

I dragged my feet. Grandfather was hauling the cedar saplings to the top of the field, where we had piled the bark slabs.

Rhoda squeezed my hand. "Don't be sad. I'll tell you everything we do."

I turned away. 'Twas *not* fair. Father knew I liked to build things. And wasn't it Rhoda who always rode to Mr. Shaw's, to see the freight wagons with their teams of glossy horses? Didn't she like to wave them off, as their harnesses jingled and sang?

Of course, just yesterday I'd wished to go with Father to the barn raising, rather than stay with Grandfather. Perhaps I was as buffle brained as Hiram, and just as foolish. I scuffed the toes of my moccasins as I followed Father, though I knew this would make him angry. 'Twas not like Father to put me in the midst of an argument. Did he wish Grandfather had never come?

And what about me? Was I glad Grandfather was here?

Yes. And no.

17. Daniel

Bump and lurch. Bump and sway. That was the dance of our wagon over the ruts, with its buck full and one rim bent. It rattled my bones till I jumped down and followed on foot to Mr. Shaw's house.

A line of wagons waited outside Mr. Shaw's barn, some pulled by oxen, others by teams of horses, one by a mule. Mr. Shaw made a list of our goods while Father chatted with other men who were sending things to the market. They talked of shillings, of pistoreens and Vermont's own currency; of our useless Continental bills. Of prices rising and falling. Of thrashing corn and winnowing wheat. Of the new cooper settled on the White River. "He makes a fine barrel," Mr. Shaw said, "useful for shipping your goods to Boston." This last was of interest to me, for I'd never seen a cooper's shop.

Their talk made me shift from foot to foot. Would we stop here all day? I thought on Grandfather and Rhoda, building a wigwam. What would it look like? Would there be room for all of us inside?

At last, the wagon was empty and Father climbed aboard. I stood in the road. "Are we going home?" I asked.

"As long as we're out, we'll stop in with Mr. Chase. See if he might mend our wheel. Hop in."

"But, Father! I promised Grandfather I'd help him."

"Enough. Your grandfather is being stubborn. He has no need to move out of the house. I offered to add on a room if he wants to stay. 'Tis a generous offer, considering we had no warning of his coming—and considering that we have no hard chink, no extra coins to rub together. Besides, you know I'm not skilled at building."

"I can help you."

"I know, and you're good at it. But this morning your place is with me. Come along."

I scrambled up and sat beside him. Father clucked to the oxen and the wagon jumped forward. "Grandfather wants his own home," I told him.

"That may be," Father said. "But he could cause trouble, building a wigwam. Trouble we don't need."

"On account of the neighbors?"

"Too many questions." Father squeezed my knee. "I'm sorry if our talk bored you. I'll try to be quick at the smithy." He tapped Jemmy's rump. The team trudged forward, their pace quickening under the lightened load.

Smoke poured from Mr. Chase's chimney. We hitched the team and went inside. Mr. Chase had a face red as his brick hearth. His shirtsleeves were rolled up, showing broad arms. He slipped a pair of iron tongs into the fire and beckoned me to the hearth. "Here's a job for you, Daniel. Pump those lungs while I look at your wagon."

The two men went outside. I took hold of the wooden handles, each one longer than my arms, and pulled the bellows together until they puffed a deep breath onto the fire. Lungs? No man or beast could have lungs so heavy to move. It took all my strength to bring the handles together. Push down, the lungs puff onto the fire. Let go and the lungs suck the air in. Out. In. Out. In. The coals blazed up. When the men came back, I had no breath of my own, but the coals were white hot.

"Good lad," Mr. Chase said. "Let it be. How old are you now, son?"

"Thirteen, sir."

"Old enough to learn a trade." Mr. Chase gave Father a long look. "Any chance he could come to me as an apprentice? He seems a good boy, and it's a fine living, being a smithy. The work will only grow, with new people moving in."

I clenched my fists in dismay.

"I think not," Father said, and I could breathe again. "His hands do steady work at home, and he's good with our animals. Besides, his mother would miss him if he were gone all day."

Mr. Chase turned his ruddy face to me. "What do you say, lad? If your mother would let you go—think you'd like to be a blacksmith?"

"No sir," I said. That fast, it came out of me.

Mr. Chase laughed. "I don't blame you," he said. "'Tis hot, hard work." He wiped his face on his sleeve and pulled a red-hot poker from the coals. *Bam! Ping! Bam!* The hammer fell on the glowing tip.

'Twas amazing to see a piece of iron bend and curve like soft wax when, just a few minutes hence, it had been hard and cold as stone. But I'd not like this work. And why did everyone talk about my future? Was this because I'd turned thirteen? If so, I wanted no part of it.

"Did you hear—the last of the prisoners kidnapped in the raid will soon come down from Canada?" Mr. Chase yelled so we could hear him above his hammering.

Prisoners? I turned to Father in alarm. Were these the ones Mrs. Ellis spoke of yesterday? I held still, listening.

"I heard of it at the barn raising," Father said.

Mr. Chase plunged the hot rod, which now boasted a hook at the end, into a kettle of water. Steam hissed and billowed as he squinted the length of the hook and shoved it back into the fire. Sweat trickled down his face. "I hope they will leave you alone," he said.

"My wife's people had naught to do with the raid, and you know it," Father said.

I wiped my palms on the seat of my breeches. I had never heard Father speak so harshly to a neighbor.

Mr. Chase swung his hammer over his head. The anvil rang out and the sound buzzed on in my ears. "Give those lungs another push or two, Daniel."

So. They didn't want me to hear? Never mind; I could fool them. I pumped the bellows slow enough to catch bits and pieces of their talk.

"Don't take me amiss," Mr. Chase said. "Your wife saved me when I burned my hand." He held up his palm, its skin puckered like an old rag. "I was ignorant of Indians myself. I know better now."

His hammering swallowed Father's reply. Then Mr. Chase said, "I hear there's a chief staying over to your place."

I held my breath, waiting for his answer. A *powwaw* wasn't a chief or a sachem. Didn't Father know that?

"Not a chief," Father said at last. "My wife's father, come to see his grandchildren." His voice rose over the racket. "I'll leave the wagon with you, come back in a day or two. Does that suit you?"

"Aye." Mr. Chase pulled a long, spiked fork from the coals. With his red cheeks, he might have been the devil that the traveling minister had preached on this summer. "Daniel, if you change your mind about working, let me know," he called. "My daughters will have naught to do with the smithy."

The cold air outside freshened my skin. In the time since we'd entered the smithy, clouds had covered the sun. I turned to Father. "Will the prisoners come to our house?"

"No," Father said. "They have no business with us. They'll want to find their families, get on with their lives, I'm sure."

I didn't believe him, but I said nothing as we loosened the traces and set the oxen free of the wagon. Father tapped Old Red on the shoulder and the oxen tripped forward. "War is an ugly business," Father said. "I'm glad it's over."

We walked on either side of the team. Jemmy tossed his head as if to shake off the yoke. I drew my coat closed. The gray sky had tucked itself over the mountains like a quilt. "Feels like snow coming," Father said.

"It snowed after the raid," I said.

Father stared at me. "You remember that? 'Twas strange, such deep snow in October."

I pulled my collar up to shield my neck, and thought of the long, cold night in the cave with Mother. We'd stepped out into fresh snow and heard Father's voice, hailing us from a great distance. "I remember you went with the militia to catch the raiders," I said. "Why did they escape?"

"'Twas a shame." Father sighed. "Our commander made us wait until first light. By then, 'twas too late. Snow covered their tracks by morning and we'd lost our chance to find them. Some called us cowards." He pushed back his hat and his eyes filled with sudden kindness. "Those prisoners must have had a time of it. I'm glad they've been released. I heard some escaped, earlier, but we've heard naught about them."

We walked without speaking. The yoke squeaked and swayed as the team hurried home. "It's too bad you heard that talk in the smithy," Father said and then, to my surprise, he laughed. "Your grandfather's hardly been here two days and the news buzzes from house to house—thanks to Mrs. Ellis, I suppose." He looked down at me. "Perhaps I did wrong, to keep you with me. Go along home; I'll stay with the oxen."

"Thank you, Father!" I took off in a rush, leaving Father and the team behind. My moccasins slapped the hardened ruts.

I ran to the gate, left it open for Father, and stopped in the foreyard to catch my breath. The curved frame of the wigwam sat atop the field. It might have been one of Mother's baskets, woven for a giant and turned upside down. Grandfather sat cross-legged, working at something in his lap. Rhoda knelt beside him.

I opened my mouth to call out—and shut it again.

A shock of yellow hair shot up from behind my grand-father. Gander Head. I nearly turned around, but Rhoda spied me and waved.

I climbed the fence and started up the hill, my feet so heavy, Mr. Chase might have filled my moccasins with iron.

18. Hiram

Pa never asked why I was gone so long and never whupped me, neither, because Ma kept us both running. She sent me to get water for cooking while Pa chopped wood. Then she wanted more water to fill the tin washtub for Uncle Abner. I fetched it, and Pa and I made a big fire outside to heat the water.

"Why ain't there a well here?" I asked Pa.

"It caved in," Pa said. "But some neighbors will help us dig it out tomorrow."

"Will Mr. Tucker come?" I asked.

Ma pursed her lips and Pa said no, not this time.

"Wish I could help you," Uncle Abner said in a hoarse voice, and then he started to cough again. He couldn't get more than three words out without a coughing fit.

"You just rest until you're better," Ma said and sent me for a cup of cider.

They kept after me all that evening and the next morning, too, cutting hemlock for another pallet, hauling water, chopping wood. Why, just the other day, Pa wouldn't let me touch the hatchet; now he sent me to use it without blinking. My blisters was raw from helping that old chief, but I didn't say nothing. I was waiting to get Uncle Abner alone.

Finally, I got my chance. After noon dinner, Uncle Abner sat outside the cabin, leaning against the logs. He had his face turned up to the sun. His cheeks was hollow, like he'd lost all his teeth. I still couldn't believe this was the same uncle who'd lived with us afore the raid.

I looked around. Ma was inside, stitching and patching the holes in my uncle's britches. Pa was up to the new well, digging with two other men. Uncle Abner and I was alone.

"Uncle Abner," I whispered.

He opened his eyes. They was rusty brown, like the dead oak leaves. "Hello, Hiram."

I looked down at him. "I saw them Injuns spear you in the raid."

"I know. And I watched them carry you off on that horse. Thought we'd never meet again. How'd you escape, anyway?"

"A woman saved me." I could see her clear as day, her black curls tossing when she faced up to that Redcoat, Lieutenant Horton. "There was a whole sight of boys," I told Abner. "The Injuns was going to carry us off to Canada, too. But this lady told the Redcoat soldier to let us go—and he did. She weren't scared of him at all."

I squatted on my heels beside him. "That lady took us back acrost the river. I left her and the other boys behind. I thought I'd find you—I swear—but a whole mess of Injuns come running right at me. I ducked into a hollow log and hid. They run right over the top a me!"

"That's some story," Uncle Abner said.

"It's true!" I said. "And there was a hawk that chased me—"

Uncle Abner held up his hands. "Enough," he said. "You

were one of the lucky ones, that's all." He shut his eyes.

"Wait." I tugged his sleeve. "Don't sleep now. There's something else." I kept my voice low. "Injuns live next door."

"Don't say. Like I said, you always was a fine storyteller."

"This ain't a story! One of them is a chief," I told him. "There's three Injuns. Four if you count the sister, but she's too little to worry about."

Uncle Abner coughed and shook his head. "Don't fool with me, boy."

"I ain't!" I said. "Ask Pa."

"Your pa wouldn't live near no Injuns," Uncle Abner said.

"But we do." I jumped up. "I'll prove it. I'll bring one of their Injun things back. Then you'll believe me."

"You do that." He begun to cough again and his face got purple. I heard Ma coming, so I slipped into the forest before she could see me.

I found my way to the edge of the Tuckers' field and hid behind the wall. The old man sat inside a curved frame, like he was in a cage. He was wrapping some kind of vine around a sapling. No sign of Daniel.

I watched a minute. What could I steal? The chief's tools looked like Pa's: a hatchet, a knife, some kind of sharp pointed thing like an awl. He had on that shiny copper jewelry, but I couldn't snatch that right off his neck. Especially not with him sitting so near to his hatchet.

"Grandfather! Hi-Rum is here!" The little girl popped up from behind the pile of slabs and runs at me with her skirts flapping. Her eyes was big and black.

I stood up, showing myself. "What are you so happy about?" I asked her. "Git."

Her mouth pulled down, but she crossed her skinny arms and didn't move.

"Rhoda," the old man called, and he said something in that other language. She run over to him. Rhoda. Was that an Injun name? Didn't sound like it.

"Yellow Hair." The old man was talking to me now. "It's good you are here. Rhoda can't lift the bark slabs, and Daniel is away with his father. You can help us."

Should I? What if he grabbed me and the voices came back? But I'd promised Uncle Abner I'd bring proof of the Injuns. Besides, I'd never seen an Injun house. So before I could say no, I was hauling slabs for the wigwam again, setting them up against the frame where the old man told me. All because I wanted to prove something to my uncle.

A while later, Daniel come trudging up the hill, his hat pulled so low I couldn't see his face. Rhoda run right to him. "Daniel, we're putting on the bark! Hiram is helping. Come see."

She swung his hand back and forth and I thought about the baby in Ma's belly. I'd never thought of having a sister. Would it be a girl?

Daniel sent me a nasty look and started hauling the slabs, same as me. I picked up two my next round, so did he. Then I tried carrying three. He did, too. Next trip, I took four slabs but dropped them and they near toppled the frame. The old man growled at us. "Be careful," he said.

I got warm. I took my coat off and laid it on a pile of brush. One of my blisters was oozing, but I didn't look at it. If Daniel could haul two or three slabs without saying a word, I could, too.

I watched the old man when no one was looking. He punched holes in the corners of the slabs and tied twine through them. "Each one overlaps the next to keep out the rain," the chief told us.

He showed us how to circle the frame with slabs, then set more on top. Soon the walls was up to my chest, then over my head. The old man tied each slab to the next one. He left a hole at the front and another one on top for the smoke to come out.

"When we're done, we'll have a fire inside," the old man said.

"It's a fast way to build a house," I said. I didn't say so, but it looked warm and dry in there. Small, but not so mean as our new place.

"You need a door," Rhoda said, "so you can stay warm."

"We can use hides," the old man said. "I hope to kill a moose or a deer this fall." He ducked in. "Come and look."

Rhoda stepped inside, but I hung back. That talk of killing made me uneasy. Daniel got on his knees and crawled after her. I was thinking whether to follow when something fell from Daniel's belt into the grass. I snatched it up and stepped away from the door so they couldn't see me.

It was a little deerskin pouch decorated with Injun designs. I slid it into my pocket just as Rhoda's head popped out. "Hiram, come in here," she said. "Grandfather will tell a story about the old ways."

I liked stories, but what were "old ways"? Some sort of Injun spells? "I don't need to see no Injun wigwam," I said. I was looking for my coat when the old man ducked under the frame and stepped up to me. He stood so close, I smelled his hot breath.

"We are Pequot people," he said. "I warned you: Don't say 'Injun' to us."

"I can talk how I want," I told him, but my heart popped against my shirt. I scooped up my coat from the brush pile, pushed one hand into the sleeve—

"Ow! Ow! Ow! I'm on fire!" Needles jabbed under my britches, up my neck, into my eye. "Stop!" I danced and swatted and stomped, but I couldn't get away. Then I heard them, buzzing and burring. Bees! "My eye, my eye!" My right eye puffed up and I couldn't see nothing.

"Be still." The old man swatted me with my jacket and pulled me away from the pile. He set his hands on my shoulders, but I couldn't stop jumping and howling. He pried my hands off my face. "Bee stings," he said. "Come to the house."

"Ow!" I yelled.

"Mother will put tobacco on them," Rhoda said.

"You did this." I hopped away and stared at them out of my good eye. Even Daniel looked sorry, but I knew the truth. "You're full of witchcraft, all a you. You made the bees sting me. And you *are* dirty Injuns, I don't care what you say. Ow! Ow!"

I ran to the woods. I couldn't hardly see the blazes on the trees, with all my blubbering. Halfway home, I dropped to the ground and touched my eye. It was swollen like an egg. I had a sting on my neck and one on my wrist, too. I took the kerchief from around my neck and rubbed my face, then jammed my hand into my pocket for the pouch.

The pain stabbed me, but I had to look. The pouch weren't much bigger than my fist. The deerskin was tied at the top with a drawstring. I opened it up. Nothing inside but bits of dried apple. I wrinkled my nose and tossed them out for the squirrels to eat. "Dirty Injun food," I said.

My stings burned and itched like the dickens and I'd left my coat behind. Never mind. I had something to show Uncle Abner. He'd have to believe me now.

19. Hiram

Ma like to have a fit when she seen my eye. "You fought with that boy! I told you to stay away. Don't we have enough problems? And where's your coat?"

Pa tipped my face up and whistled. "A real duck's egg," he said. "Tell the truth. What happened?"

"I got stung!" I danced from one foot onto the other one. "It hurts!" I showed them the other stings on my neck and my wrist, too. "Put something on it!" I begun to howl.

"Hush," Ma said. "Hiram, trouble finds you no matter where you go. Whoever heard of bees in October?"

"Don't fret," Pa said. "I'll fix him up with mud packs. He'll be fine. Come on, Hiram." Pa pushed me toward the road, tapping my shoulders like he was herding our ox. "What should we do, tie you up?" he asked. "Your ma's right—we've been here just three days and you're nothing but a nuisance."

"It's that Injun family that are pests, every one a them! They put a spell on them bees so they'd sting me!"

"Nonsense." Pa weren't having none of that. He dragged me along and paid no attention to my whimpering.

"Where we going, Pa? There's no mud along here."

"You'll see," he said.

I stumbled down the rutted road, then up another trail to a gate. I finally puzzled it out: we was coming to the Tuckers' house the proper way, instead of through the woods. Pa didn't know the shortcut.

With one eye shut tight, I banged my knee on an open door and almost fell into a dark hole.

"Steady." Pa grabbed my arm and peered over the door. "Must be their root cellar." He looked up at the house, with smoke twisting out the stone chimbley. "They have a nice place here."

Pa opened the gate and went on to the foreyard. I kept my good eye out for that nasty goose, but the barn door was shut. The dog barked inside the house. I shivered. If only I had my coat.

What was Pa doing? I dragged my feet as he went up and rapped on the door. The dog yapped louder and Daniel's ma come out. Her black hair was loose and wet, falling to her waist like a shawl.

"Good day," she said to Pa. "You must be Mr. Coombs." Before Pa could answer she looked at me, set her hand under my chin, and tipped up my head. "A bee sting," she said. "That hurts. Come inside and we'll doctor you."

'Fore I could pull away from her witchcraft, she took me into their front chamber. Daniel and his sister stared at me. They was sitting at the table board with their pa, holding quill feather pens. An inkpot sat on the table between them. Daniel's ma set me down on a bench with a tall back. "Stay here," she said. "I'll make up a poultice."

I was stuck, so I waited while Pa said good day to Mr. Tucker. The chamber was smoky and full of shadows. I wished we could go home.

"I can't see your eye," Rhoda said. "Are you blind?"

"Hush, Rhoda," Mr. Tucker said. He nodded at Pa. "Sit down and I'll bring you some cider."

"We're having lessons," Rhoda told me. She showed me her piece of bark, all covered with drippy letters. "Father told us to write this verse." She rolled the bark out flat in front of her. "Can you read it?"

"I can't see nothing outta my eye," I said. Truth is, Ma give up trying to teach me letters a while back.

Rhoda begun to read. "'Gage . . . did nothing . . . and went to pot.'" She pinched her face up and said each word slow. "'He lost . . . one town . . . another got.'"

"Who's Gage?" I asked.

"Don't you know?" Daniel said. "He was a foolish general in the war."

"A lot you know of the war," I said. We was near spitting at each other. Pa sent me a fierce look and I held my tongue.

"Perhaps Hiram could join us for lessons sometimes," Mr. Tucker said. He held out a tankard of cider to Pa, then poured one for himself.

I shook my head at Pa, but he didn't see me. He should know I'd never say yes to schooling—especially with Injuns.

Pa hemmed and hawed. "You said there might be a school in town soon?"

"We hope to build a proper one in the spring," Mr. Tucker said. "For now, I hold school here. We've no supplies, only a broken slate to write on, so I'm using birch bark. Today I made ink from iron filings, alder bark, and vinegar." He smiled at Pa.

"Who will teach us in the new school?" Rhoda asked.

Mr. Tucker tugged on his beard. "I hope I might," he said. "At least in the winter."

"You?" Daniel's voice squeaked like a rusty hinge. I tucked my chin so he wouldn't see me laugh. Course, I'd be surprised if *my* pa wanted to be the teacher. Mr. Tucker had a teacher's look, though, with wire spectacles halfway down his nose and his sleeves rolled up over his wrists.

My eye itched something fierce. I rubbed it, but that made it worse. Voices rose in the chamber behind me. Sounded like the old man and Daniel's ma speaking their strange talk. Would they make me drink an Injun potion?

Daniel's sister come over to the bench. "Father is a good teacher," she said. She showed me numbers on a slate. "We do sums, too," she said. "What's twelve plus twelve?"

"That's easy. Twenty-four," I said. From the corner of my good eye I seen Daniel counting his fingers under the table. "Give me a harder one."

Just then, the Injun woman come in carrying a mortar and pestle. The girl jumped up to look inside.

"Is it tobacco?" she asked.

"No." The woman set the mortar on the table and started to pound. "Trillium. The birth root."

"Birth root? Will it give Hi-rum a baby?" Daniel said.

Everyone laughed, even Pa. My face felt hot and I squirmed on the bench. "What's it for?" I asked.

"Don't worry." Miz Tucker smiled. She pounded that pestle up and down until the table wobbled. "Its other name is Indian balm. It will ease the pain and stop the swelling." She added drops from a brown bottle and stirred some more. Then she come over to me.

"No, don't—it'll sting!" I slid down the bench. Was she a witch?

"Be still," Pa said.

So I was. The woman rubbed something cold on my eye, then my neck and arm too, when I showed her the other stings. I was plumb surprised. They felt better right away.

"I'll wrap up the rest for you to take home," Daniel's ma said.

"Well, ma'am . . . I don't know." Pa picked up his hat and

twisted it around and around in his hands. "It's better if Hiram comes back tomorrow for another dose." He looked over at Mr. Tucker. "I weren't going to tell my wife we'd come over here. She don't believe in your kind of doctoring. I'm sorry. She don't mean no harm."

I never knew a house could be that quiet with so many people inside. Even the dog sat still, watching Pa. Miz Tucker didn't move, but her eyes looked big and dark.

I don't know what made me open my mouth. Maybe all that stillness. "Ma'am," I said, "what kind of medicine works for a cough?"

"You can chew on slippery elm bark," Rhoda said—like she was the doctress!

Daniel's ma frowned. "It depends," she said. "Do you have a cough? I didn't hear it."

"Hiram, what's got into you?" Pa said. "We don't need any more physicks." He patted his pockets. "I don't have much currency, but I've brought goods for our store. We have some real sugar cones. I'll send a piece with Hiram to-morrow, in payment for your services."

I knew Ma would be fierce if she saw Pa giving away sugar, but I didn't say a word.

"Real sugar! Daniel, won't that be fine?" Rhoda hitched over next to Daniel, but he was too busy scowling at my pa to heed her.

Pa nudged me. "Say thank you to Miz Tucker," he said.

"Thank you, ma'am," I said.

Pa hurried me out and I followed him to the gate. I didn't

show him the other path. Even though I was cold without my coat, I didn't want him to see the wigwam. Halfway to the road, I said, "I don't want to come back here."

"Why not?" Pa said. "Didn't that physick work?"

"I guess so. I still can't see nothing outta this eye."

He came close. "You can't hardly notice the poultice, so no mention of this to your mother." Pa gave me a look that meant business. "I know you were trying to help, asking about Uncle Abner's cough—but he'd never take kindly to an Indian doctress. Least, I don't think so. Let me puzzle on that awhile." He sighed. "Abner's not himself since he came back. No need to tell him about our neighbors."

Too late for that promise, so instead I asked, "Will Uncle Abner get better?"

"I don't know." Pa's shoulders sagged, like he was carrying something heavy.

I followed him up the road, my thoughts lurching from one side to another, like a wagon falling in and out a deep ruts. I was all mixed up about the Injuns. Ma told me the Injun house weren't safe, but Pa took me there and the Injun woman fixed my stings. The old man let me help with his house, then he put a spell on those bees so they'd sting me. Rhoda acted like she was my friend, but Daniel couldn't stand the sight a me. Worst of all, Injuns and Redcoats had ruint Uncle Abner and put those voices in my head.

I stopped dead in the road. I'd been in the Injun house, with all four a them. Daniel's ma had touched me with her own hands, but the voices had stayed away. Why?

I felt my pocket. That deerskin pouch was still there, pressed against my leg like a hot poultice. Should I show it to my uncle, or not? If I did, Pa would whup me for sure. If I didn't, Abner would call me a liar. Either way, I was stuck.

20. Daniel

Father closed the door, pulled in the latchstring, and gathered our school things. He set the quill pens, the ink, and the bark on the shelf beside the hornbook. "Lessons are over," he said.

"Why?" Rhoda asked. "We didn't do our sums."

I was glad of that, but I didn't say so. Writing is hard, but sums are even harder. It shamed me to hear Hiram so quick with them. And he'd seen me counting on my fingers, even with his bad eye.

Father stepped close to Mother. "I'm sorry, Kate," he said. "Mrs. Coombs may cause us trouble."

"Yes, I thought so." Mother used her fingers to comb through her tangles. She twisted the long strands into a braid as she spoke to me. "This is why you don't like Hiram?"

I nodded, and bent to stroke Jody's ears. I couldn't meet Mother's eyes.

"Daniel." Her hand settled on my shoulder. "'Tis not Hiram's fault."

I stood up so fast I almost knocked the bench over. "I don't care. He's a cruel, gander-headed—"

"Daniel." Father's voice stopped me. "Enough."

I looked from Mother to Father. Though one was dark, the other fair; one short, the other tall; one stocky, the other thin—in this, they were of one mind, a wall before me.

"Hiram helped us with the wigwam," Rhoda said.

Even my sister! Would everyone take Gander Head's side? "Grandfather told the bees to sting him because he called us a bad word," Rhoda said.

"Nonsense," Father said. "Bees do what they like." He pushed the coals against the big backlog. "No more talk of the neighbors." He waved at me. "The kindling basket is empty. Best get on with your chores."

I bent to Rhoda as I lifted the basket. "When I come back, I'll work at your doll," I whispered. "I won't be gone long."

I went outside. Nothing was right since the Coombs family settled in on the hill. They had spoiled everything—even Grandfather's visit.

I sat on my stump in the shed, set a log on end, and hoisted my froe. I hammered it into the log with the splitting club Father had made for me.

"Ouch!" I dropped the club after one blow. The splinter was hot in my palm, and I'd a blister on the other hand. Still, the log broke open along the grain. I set it on end and gritted my teeth, ready to split the log again, when the shed darkened. Grandfather stood in the doorway, blocking the light.

"Watch your blisters." He took the froe and the club and sat in my place on the stump. "Let me split while you fill the basket." He smiled, showing blackened teeth at the back of his mouth. "In our village, this was always a job for the old men and the boys," he said. *Thwack!* The froe set into the wood. *Thwack!* The log opened into many pieces, like the petals of a flower. I gathered the kindling and set it in the basket. We set up a steady rhythm. *Thwack!* Clatter. *Thwack!* Clatter. Scoop and gather.

"What kind of tree is best for the canoe?" I asked, as I tucked my pieces into the basket.

"So you are still planning a dugout." Grandfather studied me. "You must find a straight tree with no branches." *Thwack!* "A chestnut will last forever."

"How do we make the canoe?" I asked.

Grandfather set the froe across his knee. "Listen well."

I hunkered down beside him. "I'm listening."

"First peel off the bark. Then build a fire inside the log and watch it carefully. Burn it, and scoop out the wood. It takes a long time."

"Will it be ready when snowmelt fills the rivers?" I asked.

"If you work hard."

"I will." I frowned. Grandfather spoke as if I'd be working alone.

"Where will you take it?" he asked.

I'd not thought on that. "Down to the river, to fish. I'll catch all the trout I want—and no Yellow Hair to steal them from me."

Grandfather frowned. "Does Yellow Hair steal?"

"Yes, and then lies about it after."

"The demons again," Grandfather said. I wanted to protest, but Grandfather went on. "A river dugout can be small; just big enough for two men to paddle. Years ago, Pequots crossed to Long Island in enormous dugouts. Those canoes held more men than the fingers on both hands." He held up his hands, but they trembled, and he drew them quickly to his sides.

"The canoe should be big enough for three," I said. "You, me, and Rhoda." I took a deep breath. "Grandfather, I don't want that Gander Head to help us."

Grandfather's laugh was like a dry cough. "Don't worry. The work is too hard and boring for Yellow Hair."

"But not for me."

Grandfather raised his eyebrows and said nothing. I stood tall, my shoulders back. Though my back and arms ached, I'd worked hard all day, hadn't I? "Can we look for a tree tomorrow, after we finish the wigwam?"

Grandfather made a grunting sound. That meant *maybe*. I crossed my arms and hugged myself. I was beginning to puzzle out my grandfather's language—the one that was neither Pequot nor English.

Sentinel

A flock of crows
wheels,
batters the sky,
and lands
in the bleached stalks
of the cornfield,
sounding their raucous chorus
of complaint.
One crow sits
watching.

Perched on the twisted limb
of an oak
his gaze hints of a smile.
He keens a warning
when a woman runs at the flock,
arms flailing;
raises his voice—
Caw! Caw!—
when a fox slinks toward them,
tail bristling.

On guard,
the crow's ebony eye
snares

a rabbit scuttling through dry grass;
a boy with yellow hair,
hands cupping his ears,
crouching behind a haycock;
a dark-haired boy
crossing the pasture
whose moccasins
fall   without a sound.

A wind rises,
thrashing in the branches,
and a man stumbles into the open,
red hair matted,
fist raised.
The crow sounds the alarm.
As one, the flock lifts into a cold rain:
a black cloud of beating wings.

The sentinel
misses nothing:
not the crimson bead from the woman's skirt
settling into a furrow like a seed;
nor the porcupine quill
shining in the dark soil;
nor the last kernel of corn
left behind as a gift
for his patience.

The crow sinks,
snatches the sweet morsel,
pushes into the wind,
and joins his flock
in the surging branches
of the hemlocks;
settles on an outer limb,
black eye gleaming—

and waits.

Part III

❧

Whistling in the East

21. Hiram

I should a known Ma would find out about the doctress. First she sniffed at the cider on Pa's breath. "Where you been?" she asked. "Night's coming on, and not a stick of wood in the house. I can't hardly bend over and I've got the sick headache. I had to send Abner out, lame as he is—and you're off drinking with the neighbors?"

"I'll fetch some wood," I said. I tried to slip past her big belly, but she grabbed my sleeve and pulled me close. "What's that on your face?" she asked. "Tell me." Her fingernails dug into my skin through my shirt.

"It's a poultice," I said.

She gave Pa such a cold stare, I thought he might ice over right on the spot. "You took him to that witch. Didn't you?"

"She fixed it so it don't hurt no more," I said.

Ma hauled off to slap me. I dodged outta the way just in time and bumped into Uncle Abner. He was coming in the door with his arms full a wood. The logs clattered to the floor; one landed on my foot, and I yelped.

"Hey!" Uncle Abner said. "Watch out." He kicked the log

away. He was wearing Pa's old boots. "Come on," he told me. "Help me pick these up."

"Just wait," Ma said. "All a you." She was breathing funny.

Pa held up his hand. "Now, Hannah—don't cause trouble."

When Ma's face gets splotchy and red like her hair, there's no use saying a word. Don't Pa know that? I sure do. I grabbed the spilt logs and stacked them by the hearth, keeping as far away as I could.

Pa put his arm acrost her shoulders, trying to calm her down, but Ma shoved him right off. "You don't want Abner to know, do you?"

"Know what?" my uncle said.

"That we live next door to savages, that's what," she said.

"Hannah!" Pa shouted. I covered my ears. Pa's voice is usually quiet, compared to Ma's.

Uncle Abner's face twisted up. "So my nephew told the truth," he said. "Ain't that a pretty picture. Injuns torch my house, kill our cattle, kidnap me, and take me to Canada. I spend two years in a British prison, nearly die tunneling outta that jail, almost starve to death getting back over the border, and you tell me there's Injuns next door?" He coughed so hard he slumped against the doorpost while Pa slapped his back.

Uncle Abner clutched my sleeve. "Come on," he said. "Show me the way."

Ma begun to holler. I didn't know what she was saying. Pa was shouting even louder. "Abner, calm down. These folks had nothing to do with that raid. The husband is an Englishman—"

"English! Damnation on those Redcoats!" Abner roared at Pa. "They's even worse than the Indians. They treated their swine better than us." Uncle Abner shook me. "And you said there's a chief over there. What's he got planned for us?"

I couldn't answer him. I kept my hands over my ears. All three of them commenced to shout and yell at each other and at me.

My teeth was chattering and it come over me again: The roaring. Horses squealing and stampeding up the riverbed. Me let loose from the Injun, running alone through the forest. More Injuns coming at me, carrying kettles and guns from our house. Smoke like fog in the forest, choking my lungs. No place safe.

I twisted out from Abner and bolted.

Run to the timber. Run through the rain. Into the woods. Dodge the trees, duck from that hawk, find the rotten log. The log you can hide under. Scuttle in. Hold still.

Stop your bawling. Don't breathe. Don't scream. Freeze while they run over the top of you, footsteps pounding. Don't cry out, don't shake, don't flinch.

Hide. Hide. Hide.

22. Daniel

Rhoda woke me in the night, crying. She fixed on one word I couldn't understand, saying it over and over. I shook her.

"Rhoda, wake up. You're dreaming." She pulled away. Her sobs brought whimpers from Jody below.

I heard footsteps, then the ladder's creak. I turned over, expecting Mother, but Grandfather's low voice came from the darkness. He stood near the top rung and rubbed my sister's back, crooning a song as soothing as one of Mother's salves. Rhoda's sobs faded, but Grandfather kept on singing. I pulled the blankets up around my ears and let the song carry me away, down into the dark, warm cave where sleep waited.

I woke to the *thump, thump, thump* of Mother's mortar, keeping a steady beat with the rain. Though the loft was dark, I needed the privy, so I left the warmth of my blankets. Rhoda stirred, but her eyes stayed shut.

The shed was cold. I returned to the front chamber and stood by the fire, half asleep. Mother sat on her stool. Her arms lifted and fell. Lifted and fell. The pestle rose, then thumped down on the kernels, turning them to meal. She gripped the mortar tight between her knees to keep it still. She smiled at me, but her arms kept up their rhythm.

Grandfather sat at the table, cutting kernels from the cob with Mother's rounded corn scraper. "Good morning, Grandfather," I said. He didn't greet me.

"My father is angry at me," Mother said, but she winked. "He says it is women's work to prepare the *waweekanash*— the cob corn."

"She makes me do it, too," I told him. A smile tugged at Grandfather's mouth. I held my hands to the flames, but they wouldn't warm. More thumping came from the barn. "What is Father doing?" I asked.

"Mending the sheepfold," Mother said.

I liked working beside Father in the barn, smelling the warmth of the animals and listening to their small noises, but this morning I couldn't move. A gust of wind chased smoke back down the chimney and into my eyes. I coughed and waved the smoke away. Raindrops sizzled on the hearth. I turned to Grandfather. "Will we finish the wigwam today?" I asked.

Grandfather shrugged. "Only if the rain stops."

Rhoda stood beside me, her fingers in her mouth. I started. She had slipped into the room with the silence of a cat.

Mother's arms went still and the pestle fell sideways. Grandfather set the corn aside. "Come sit by me," he said. Rhoda sat on the bench, her bare feet dangling. Mother wrapped her in a shawl and sat on the other side. I watched. What was this?

"A dream came to you," Grandfather said.

Rhoda sat up straight, her black eyes gleaming.

"Do you remember your dreams?" I asked her. Mine always swam away, like trout fingerlings slipping through holes in the fish weir.

"I was a hawk," Rhoda said. "I was carried on the east wind."

I stared. My sister's face hardened with the bird's fierce gaze.

"What kind of hawk?" Grandfather asked.

"The one that told us you were coming," Rhoda said. "I was big, with a red tail. I flew over the wheat field."

"The red-tailed hawk." Mother gave the bird its Pequot name, and I recognized the word Rhoda had cried in her sleep.

"There was a storm," Rhoda said. "The east wind caught me and threw me too high, up above our barn. The wind whistled." Her voice trembled. Mother pulled her close. Rhoda's eyes fixed on our tiny window and I followed her gaze. What did she find there? I saw only the rain, lashing against the shutters.

"I hated the whistling. There was thunder. And lightning beyond the mountains," Rhoda said. "Mother and Father were gone. They didn't live here anymore." Her sobs had come back.

"Rhoda, 'twas but a dream—"

"Ssst!" Mother put up her hand to me. "Let her finish."

"I flew so high I couldn't come down." Rhoda gulped. "I thought I would stay in the sky forever."

"But you didn't," Mother said. "You're here, in our chamber."

Rhoda sobbed against Mother's chest. What foolishness. "If you were a hawk, why were you scared?" I asked. "Hawks love to fly."

"Be still," Mother said. Though she hadn't touched me, I felt slapped. Mother and Grandfather gave each other strange looks over Rhoda's head. Speaking without saying a word. When they finally spoke, it was in Pequot, and so soft

I could barely hear. I made out some talk of *powwaws,* and dreams, and of the whistling from the east, but the thrumming of the rain hid the rest from me.

I could have touched Mother, or my sister, but I didn't. Though they were near me in the chamber, they might have flown off across the river and beyond the mountains. If being a *powwaw* brought nightmares and weeping, I wanted no part of it.

At last, Rhoda's sobs quieted. I took up my knife, found the piece of soft pine I'd set aside for her doll, and sat near the fire. "Look, Rhoda," I said. "I'm going to shape your doll now. Do you want a boy or a girl?"

She wiped her eyes on her sleeve. "Girl," she said.

"All right. She needs a name."

"First I have to see what she looks like." Rhoda slid off Mother's lap and settled beside me on the bench. Her back shuddered with her last tears. Mother pulled stockings onto Rhoda's bare feet and touched my hair so gently, it seemed that a feather from the hawk had settled there, then floated away.

I worked with care. Fresh curls of pine fell to the floor. Raindrops sizzled on the fire as the doll took shape. Blocky head, short neck, long body. I turned the pine over and over. How to show the arms and legs? How to give her a skirt? That would be difficult. I gripped the bone handle too hard and winced.

"Ow." I set the knife down and sucked on the splinter in my hand, with its hot swelling.

"What is it?" Rhoda asked. "Let me see."

"A sliver. From making the frame for the wigwam."

Rhoda took my hand in her small one and turned my palm up. Her eyes so serious—like Mother's when she visits a sick person—studied the sore. She touched it with her fingertip and I flinched. "Don't."

"Mother, look," Rhoda said. "Daniel's hand is hot."

I wanted to hide it, but Mother pried my fingers open. "You must soak it in hot water," she said, "and then I will pull it out."

"But, Mother—"

"Be still." She poured steaming water from the kettle on the hob and set a bowl in front of me. "Sit by the fire while Grandfather and I chop apples for apple butter."

Grandfather groaned. "Another job for women. She makes me work too hard." He gave me a sly wink.

Mother tested the water in the bowl and added a little cold water from the pitcher. "Try it now."

"Too hot!" I drew my hand out, then slowly dipped it in again. In and out; in and out, until the heat suited me.

Rhoda peeled apples and Mother chopped them. The sweet smell tickled my nose. "I've a relish for food," I said. "We've not eaten."

"Your belly has a hole in the bottom," Mother said. "Take a piece of jonnycake while I pluck out the splinter." She held my hand and squeezed the palm, then picked at it with a needle.

"Ow! I can't eat while you stick me!" I tried to pull away, but Mother held on tight.

"Look the other way," she said.

Mother was right: when I didn't watch, it hurt me less. "Done," she said. She held up a long sliver. "Now you can eat."

The bread was dry and cold, but I gobbled it anyway, then cast about for more.

"*Chahnameed,*" said Grandfather.

"What's that?" I asked.

"A Mohegan story," Grandfather said.

"Tell us!" Rhoda bounced on the bench, nearly tipping over my bowl.

"A story is fine on a dark day." Father had come into the chamber. He hung his dripping coat and hat on a peg and stood by the fire. Steam rose from his wet breeches. "Will you share it with us?" he asked.

Wegun! Father was showing kindness to Grandfather. I hugged my arms across my chest to hold on to my smiles.

Grandfather looked at Mother. "In long-ago days, night was the best time for sharing stories and lessons," he said, "and then, only after the hard frosts had come."

"But Jack Frost has bitten us very hard now," I told him.

Grandfather nodded. "True. And this morning is as dark as candle-lighting time." He smiled at me. "*Chahnameed's* story will suit you, Daniel."

He sat on the stump by the fire, flicked his long braid

143

over his shoulder, bowed his head, and was silent. The wind whined in the chimney and Jody answered it with a growl. "Shh," I whispered. I stroked her ears, soft as deerskin.

"*Chahnameed* was a trickster," Grandfather said. "And a glutton. Always hungry." He raised an eyebrow at me.

"I'm not!" But in truth, his teasing pleased me.

"There was an eating match," Grandfather said, "but *Chahnameed* was clever. He hid a bag under his shirt, with the opening near his mouth. He pretended to pour the food into his mouth. No one could see that the food went into the bag."

"What happened?" Rhoda asked. The fear had vanished from her eyes.

"*Chahnameed* and another man slurped their soup," Grandfather said. "They ate barley. Then *sauthauthig*—Indian pudding. Then *yokeg*—jonnycakes. So much food, the other man was groaning, like this." Grandfather bent over, clutched his stomach, and moaned, "Ooo-aggh!"

Everyone laughed, even Father.

"Of course, *Chahnameed* poured everything into his bag," Grandfather said, "but the other man didn't know. Soon he was too full to eat another bite!" Grandfather rolled his eyes and held his stomach again. "So *Chahnameed* won."

I jumped up. "I don't eat like *Chahnameed!*"

Grandfather's smile showed all the way to his blackened teeth. "No," he said. "I was only teasing. You are growing, just as your father says."

Wegun again! Now Grandfather was showing kindness to Father. Had they finished fighting?

"Was that the end of the story?" Mother asked.

Before Grandfather could answer, the sun stuck his long fingernail through a crack in the shutters.

"Look." I opened the shutters. Now the sun shone his whole face into the chamber. "*Chahnameed* the trickster brought the sun back. The rain has stopped." I hurried to find my coat and beckoned to Grandfather. "May we finish the wigwam? Rhoda, find your boots."

"Daniel," said Mother, "you interrupted your grandfather's story. And I need to bandage your hand."

"'Tis fine," I said.

Grandfather waved us away. "The story is done," he said. "I'll follow when we finish the apples."

I wanted to hug Grandfather, but I felt too shy. "Will you tell us another story later?" I asked. In truth, I didn't hear his reply. Coat buttoned, laces tied, hat on—I was ready.

"Wait for me!" Rhoda wriggled into her boots, then tripped to Father to lace them up. I went out and stood in the foreyard, waiting. The wind swirled leaves and straw chaff in a dizzy dance. I touched my belt. The knife was there—but where was Mother's pouch? I searched my coat pockets, then my breeches. Empty. Had I left it at the wigwam?

"Close the door!" Father called.

I slammed it shut and Rhoda took my hand. We ran up the hill, leaning into the wind as it tried to push us back to the house. The grass was slick from the rain. A sharp gust nearly knocked us down, and Rhoda screamed.

"What's wrong?" But then I saw. The sentinel oak atop the

hill waved its branches over empty ground. The wigwam was gone.

"Did it blow away?" Rhoda whispered. We crept up the hill, holding each other tight.

The wigwam lay open like a barrel missing its staves. Slabs of bark, which we had cut and fastened with such care, were strewn across the ground in every direction.

I tasted sour jonnycake in my throat. Rhoda began to cry. "The storm knocked it down because of my dream," she said.

"No." I pulled her close. She was so innocent. So little. But I must tell her. "Not the dream, or the storm," I said. "Look." I showed her the twine, slashed into ribbons. "Someone cut it apart on purpose."

Rhoda shivered against me. "Who?"

"I don't know. We'd best tell Grandfather."

"Wait!" We turned to hear a high voice calling through the wind.

A yellow head popped up from behind the wall. "You!" I cried. Gander Head's eye was still big as an egg, his hair full of twigs and bark, breeches and shirt soaked through. "*You* did this. This time, I *will* dust your back!" I leapt at him, my fists raised.

"No!" Hiram danced away. "I didn't! I got caught in the storm. I come for my coat and to get more medicine for my stings, like your ma told me! I swear." He snatched his wet jacket, lying on the brush pile.

Rhoda grabbed my sleeve, yanked me so hard I nearly toppled. "Stop," she said. "Don't fight."

I twisted away from her. "But Hiram did it! He hates us so much, he had to tear it down." I lunged at him. "Stupid Gander Head!" Hiram dodged and I stumbled. I fell on my sore hand and spoke an oath.

Rhoda jumped between us as I found my feet. She put her skinny arms out—as if she could stop us! Still, we both backed away. "Hiram didn't do it," Rhoda said. She looked at him. "Did you?"

"No. I'll swear on Ma's Bible," Hiram said. Then his mouth twisted into that nasty sneer. "Guess you don't even know what a Bible is."

"We do, too," I snapped. "And what's the good of your having one? You can't even read it!"

What was this—a tear leaking from that sorry eye? Had I made him cry? One moment, he was fuming and fussing, and the next he was gone, over the wall and into the forest. The air spat out of me in a rush, like Mr. Chase's bellows. I felt unsettled, and not just because of the wigwam.

"Poor Grandfather," I said.

Rhoda turned her face up to me. "'Twas not Hiram," she said again.

"How do you know?"

"He was afraid," she said. "And he helped us build it—though he doesn't even like to work." She gave me a half smile.

"Then who was it?"

Rhoda pointed at the wet ground. Tracks. I should have thought on that myself. I dropped to my knees. My breeches were soaked in a moment. Footprints ran back and forth in the mud between the wheat stubble. "Here's my moccasin. Is this your boot?"

Rhoda set one foot in the track, and it matched. She pointed to more tracks, pressed into the soft mud. "This is Hiram," she said. "He walks with his toes turned in. Like a duck."

"Or like a gander!" I laughed. "You're so smart."

And what were these? My fingers traced a bigger track, then a second. I stood and followed them. Across the furrows. Around the wigwam and into the meadow ground. I felt the tracks with my fingertips, as Mother had shown me long ago. Each boot print was filled with small, deep holes. "Someone else was here," I said. "Someone big. With hobnails in his boots."

"Who?" Rhoda's hood fell back and the wind whipped fear across her face, darkened her black eyes.

"I don't know. Run to Grandfather, and bring Jody. I'll wait for you here."

23. Daniel

Grandfather's chin quivered when he saw the wigwam, its pieces scattered atop the hill like the bones of a deer picked clean by wolves. Wind came at us in gusts and Grandfather swayed, an old tree about to fall. I held his arm and Mother took his elbow. We made a wall around him. "We can fix it," I said. "It won't take long."

Father spoke a nasty oath and flung down his hat. Anger flushed his face above his beard. He shook a fist at the forest. "We won't stand for this!"

Jody whimpered and scurried off with her tail between her legs. I caught my breath, and Rhoda's fingers went into her mouth. Father never swore.

"It must be Coombs," Father said. "I thought I could trust him."

Hiram's father? Would he do such a thing? "Rhoda and I studied the tracks," I said. "It's a man wearing hobnail boots."

"Yes." Grandfather nodded at me, then dropped to his knees. I watched him finger the tracks, watched the trembling of his hands. Had they been so unsteady when he came, or was it the shock?

"Hobnail Boots walks with a limp," Grandfather said. He beckoned to me. "See? Put your hands in the tracks, one on this side, one on the other." I did as he asked. The mud was cold under my hands. One track sank deeper than the other.

"He came from the road," I said, "and then across the meadow ground." I pointed to the muddy ruts and the tracks coming up from the haycocks.

Grandfather nodded. "Your mother's teachings have served you well."

His praise warmed me. I glanced at Father, to see if he

heard, but he was bent over the tracks. "Mr. Coombs doesn't limp, does he?" Father asked. "Think, Kate. Have you doctored anyone with a bad leg or a wound?"

"No." Mother sighed. "Everyone needs physick for the canker rash, the putrid throat."

Rhoda squatted by Hiram's tracks. "Hiram was here when we came," she said.

"Hiram!" Father picked up his hat and dusted it off. "He's a menace. And slippery as a greased sow. Coombs is right: the boy deserves a good scolding. Perhaps he led Hobnail Boots to the wigwam."

"Hiram didn't do it," Rhoda said.

"No." Grandfather stepped over the tracks, taking care not to spoil them. "But maybe Yellow Hair knows something." He picked up a length of twine. "Hobnail Boots has cut all my fastenings with a knife or a hatchet. We must be careful—he is full of fury."

Grandfather faced Father. The wrinkles on his face seemed more deeply scored, as if carved with my knife. "Perhaps I was wrong to come," he said. "I have brought trouble to your family."

Mother put her arm around his waist. "You are *in* our family," she said. "This is your home, too."

Father held his hat in his hands. "Kate is right," he said. "And I did not greet you properly when you came. I owe you my life, and you are grandfather to my children. You're always welcome here."

Grandfather and Father shook hands and nodded their

heads as if they were taking a vow. I swallowed tears and pulled my jacket close over my chest. A cold wind sliced through the wool until I shivered.

"Winter is coming on," Mother told Grandfather. "The house will be warm. Live inside with us, and we will rebuild the wigwam in the spring."

I stood up tall. "No," I said. "We should fix it for him now."

"I agree," said Father, "but first we must be sure your grandfather is safe—that everyone is safe here on our hillside."

"Will they break our house down, too?" Rhoda asked.

"Of course not," Father said. A shadow slid across his face. Our own father—who never seemed to fear anything—looked sorely troubled.

Would the man who ruined the wigwam tear down our house next? Would it be like the raid, but with everything backward: whites chasing Indians this time, whites burning our houses, killing our cattle, stealing *us* away, even though the war had ended? I looked down the hill. Smoke twisted from our chimney. The sheep huddled in their stone pen, their rumps turned to the wind. The gander pecked the wet grass in the foreyard, and the last of the corn rattled in the cold gusts sweeping up from the valley. Could we lose our home?

"We must not tarry," Father said. "We will catch the man who did this if we have to check every boot in Griswold."

Who could it be? I stared at the tracks and noticed something. I glanced at Grandfather, but he was speaking with Father.

"I'll go to the Ellises," Father said. "They'll help to start a search."

"I'll come with you," Grandfather said.

"We'll start the rebuilding," Mother said. "Daniel, Rhoda, come to the barn to fetch the tools."

"I'll stay and gather the shingles," I said, dropping my eyes to the ground. Mother must not catch me out in this lie.

"Be careful," Mother said.

"I will. Jody, bide with me." I kept Jody close while Mother and Rhoda went down the path. The wind whipped their skirts and tugged at their shawls. My heart was heavy. I feared for us all. And in spite of what everyone said, I couldn't hold Gander Head blameless. How could I?

"Look, Jody." I squatted in the midst of the scattered slabs and pulled Jody's nose to Hobnail's track. She sniffed and quivered. "Grandfather was right that Hobnail Boots came from the road," I told her. "But he didn't notice that the tracks do not return to the road. They go into the timber. Toward Hiram's."

I hoisted two shingles and set them aside. Hobnail's tracks circled the place where the wigwam had sat, then zigzagged toward the wall, like those of a man who has swallowed too much cider.

Jody growled and sniffed the wind. "What's wrong, girl?" I squinted at the house. Mother and Rhoda stood in the foreyard, speaking to Mrs. Ellis. Why was she here again?

Perhaps about her niece with the canker rash. Good. If she needed more of Mother's physicks, that gave me more time. I snapped my fingers at Jody and pushed her nose close to Hobnail's tracks. "Here, girl. Smell these and remember the scent. Now find him. Go!"

Jody snuffled at the wet ground and wagged her tail. She veered toward Hiram's pigeon-toed markings, but I called her back. "Not those—the big ones." I held her nose to them again. Now she understood. Her nose skimmed the ground as she loped along, and I dashed to follow her.

We ran to the edge of the wheat field. Over the wall, into the forest, across the felled log. Heart in my throat. Lungs near bursting. Hobnail Boots had used a hatchet to cut the twine, or a knife. What if he were hiding, waiting, behind this spruce tree—or that oak—or the speckled boulder? My belly lurched and twisted. I willed my moccasins to silence; ran swift and kept to the soft parts of the trail, away from small sticks that could snap and announce my presence.

On the far side of the stream, where the trail led to Hiram's house, Jody stopped. She trotted back and forth, as if her nose followed the spokes of a wheel, coming back to the center, then out again.

"What's wrong?" I dropped to one knee. The trail grew faint, lost in the carpet of wet leaves. "Did he go to Hiram's?"

Jody whined, then took off for Mr. Coombs's woodlot, glancing at me over her shoulder. Her amber eyes said: *This way.*

I caught her up. "Are you sure?" I whispered. Behind me, the sighing of the wind, and the safety of my family. Ahead of me, danger. Should I go on? Mother would worry, finding the hilltop empty. But if I caught Hobnail Boots—wouldn't they be glad?

"All right," I told Jody. "Let's go."

She dashed away, nose hugging the wet ground, ears flopping like small flags. "Jody, wait!" My voice echoed in the forest. Buffle brain! I had forgotten to keep quiet.

A hole opened in the forest canopy, and a patch of blue sky drew my eye. We were close to the woodlot. Jody stopped, stiffened, and growled. I came even with her and grabbed her collar. Her neck fur bristled beneath my hand.

"What is it?" I whispered.

She snarled. A cough, the deep cough of a man, answered from the clearing.

"Hsst." I kept a strong hold on her collar and inched forward, careful not to show myself. Jody growled again. I clapped a hand over her muzzle, but too late.

"Who's there? Show yourself."

'Twas a man's voice, almost the snarl of an animal—and not a voice I knew. My palms were wet in spite of the cold.

Branches snapped. Jody barked and lunged. I stood up, keeping hold of her, as a man limped toward us. My legs jellied, my bones had gone soft. The man's rusty hair lay matted on his shoulders, his eyes wild and staring. I took a quick glance at his feet. Yes, he wore heavy boots. The man raised a hatchet and shook it at me. Jody went wild. I strained to hold her.

"Well, well," the man said. "What have we here? One of them dirty Injuns Hiram warned me about." He raised the hatchet. "I've got a score to settle with you people."

"Don't touch me." I took a few steps back. Jody lunged against her collar, barking and choking. "I'll let my dog loose on you."

"Just try it." The man staggered toward me, then doubled over in a fit of coughing that liked to kill him. His face was near purple, and the hatchet dangled from his hand.

My only chance. I let loose of Jody and kicked the hatchet. It went flying, the sharp blade catching the sun. Jody's snarling was fierce and she went at his breeches as if to tear them to shreds. The man howled.

"Jody, down!" I grabbed her and pulled her with me. "Come after me. Run!"

I dashed into the forest, dragging Jody at first, then letting her loose when we'd left the clearing behind. This time, I had no care for silence, and I durst not look behind me, for fear he followed. My feet led me to the steep banks of the hemlock ravine, a place I thought I'd never see again. I slid under the feathery branches, down to the *sneeksuck,* the cave beneath the ledge where Mother had tucked us away the night of the raid.

I scrambled in, my breath coming in gasps, and pulled Jody to me for warmth and comfort. When my breathing slowed, I looked around. Had it been so cramped? How did we all fit? But of course: we were smaller then, Rhoda so young she rode on Mother's back down the hill, her legs wrapped around Mother's waist.

I curled up tight now, hugging Jody, and thought on that night. The three of us had huddled together while musket shots peppered the hills and screams clawed their way up the valley. The legs of a man had flashed near us, his feet wrapped in moccasins. He passed so close we might have touched him if we'd reached out from beneath the rock. And I remembered something else—

A hawk.

I let loose of Jody as it came back to me. A red-tailed hawk had flown over us. Mother followed her down the bank and across the brook until she came on this ledge. Had the hawk showed us the way? Was it the same hawk that spoke to Rhoda before Grandfather came? Mother said they claimed the same nest every year. Did the hawk remember us?

Jody's wet nose pushed against my neck. I stroked her and listened hard. No sound but the wind's sigh, and the steady song of the brook. "It's done, girl," I said. "We escaped. Good dog."

The ugly man had said he had a score to settle. What did he mean?

I thought on Mr. Chase in the smithy, telling Father about prisoners come down from Canada. Was this one of those men?

Cold shadows crept into the ravine. I scrambled out from

beneath the ledge. A stitch tugged at my side, but I crossed the brook and kept my head down, parting the branches of the hemlocks before me as I climbed the hill. I must warn them before 'twas too late.

24. Hiram

When I first saw the wigwam broke up, with the bark slabs laying on the ground, I was all mixed up. I thought how I helped to carry them shingles to the sledge, how I set them on end and held them in place while the old man tied them to the poles. I never did get to go inside. Truth is, I liked the looks of it. I wanted to sit in there when no one was around. No one would scold me, or send me out for wood or water. I'd build myself a fire and watch the smoke drift out the hole at the top. But of course, I'd never go in now, even if they fixed it up again. Not after the things I'd said about Injuns— Indians, I mean.

I shouldn't a run when Ma and Pa was yelling. I should a stayed, taken Pa's belt, tried to stop Uncle Abner. Too late now. My uncle had gone and wrecked the wigwam. I'm sure I seen him run off in the rain. Anyway, who else would a done it?

They'd come after him for sure. Daniel was right—I was to blame, in a way. If only I'd never told Uncle Abner about Daniel's family in the first place.

So now the wigwam was broke. I stumbled home, my eye

still swollen because I durst not ask for more physics. I took my time going back, but finally hunger made a noise in my belly. I couldn't stay in the forest all night, could I? Not with those wolves howling on the ridge at night. At least Pa would keep us safe, even if he wanted to whup me.

But what was this? No sounds in the clearing. The door closed. No smoke from the chimbley.

I opened the door slow and careful. "Ma?"

No answer. "Pa? Uncle Abner?"

Where did they go? Was Ma having her baby somewhere?

I went outside. No sign of the cart. Uncle Abner's ox was gone. The rope dangled from the branch where we'd tied him. Did they leave me? The fire was out, no food in sight. I plunked myself on my pallet and bawled.

I must a cried myself to sleep. I woke near dusk and heard voices down by the road. They was coming back! I went out to meet them but pulled up short.

It weren't none of my family, but Daniel's pa and grandpa, with two strangers, standing right in our foreyard. One was Pa's age, the other must a been his son. They was both clean shaven, with Adam's apples that gave them rooster necks. I looked them over careful. They wasn't carrying guns, least none that I could see. What could they want?

"Hello, Hiram," Mr. Tucker said. "Is your father at home?"

"No sir. No one here but me." That was the truth, anyway.

He frowned. "Do you know who destroyed our wigwam?"

I clenched my fists. "Not me!"

The old man stepped close. "Be still, Yellow Hair. I know you didn't do it."

"You do?" I was surprised. I thought the old man would blame me for sure.

"Perhaps you can say who did," he said.

"I don't know nothing." I was twitching all over, and for once I couldn't find a story to tell. Still, I wasn't *sure* of Uncle Abner being up there. I was only guessing.

"My name is Ellis," said the man behind Mr. Tucker. "This is my son, Timothy. We have the farm just down the road. Mind if we come in?"

"No one's here." I stood in the path. They could push past me if they wanted—and, sure enough, the younger one did.

"I'll just have a look." He went to the house and took hold a the latch like he lived there.

"Wait," I said. "You got no right to come in. Pa says don't open the door to strangers."

"Your pa is right," Mr. Tucker said. "But there's no need to worry. These are your neighbors."

What could I do? There was four of them and one of me. I watched while they poked around inside. It must have seemed shabby to them, with the stump in the middle, the fire cold, and Ma and Pa's store goods piled up in the corner, the barrels and burlap bundles still unpacked.

"See?" I said. "No one's here. I don't know where they went, Ma or Pa or Uncle Ab—" Fool! My face went red. There. I'd gone and done it. Too late to swallow my words.

"Uncle?" Mr. Tucker give me a funny look then. "Your uncle lives here?"

"No sir. He's just . . . visiting," I said. That was true, weren't it? I tried to keep my voice from trembling so much. "He might a gone home."

"Where's that?" the one called Timothy asked.

I thought fast. "Downriver."

"Downriver where?" Mr. Ellis asked.

I shrugged. "I can't say. We just moved here."

"I'm sure you must know his name," the younger Ellis man said.

Now I was stuck. "Abner," I said.

"Abner who?" Timothy asked.

I held my tongue and glanced toward the road. Still no sign of Ma or Pa, and the sun going down. Where were they?

"You'd better go now," I said.

Mr. Tucker give me a long look. "Come along to our house," he said. "You've got no fire, and night's coming on. We can leave your folks a message."

"Pa don't like me running off." Truth is, I was skairt. What if Ma and Pa had left me for good? What if Ma had gone to find a doctor and she was too sick to come home? What if that wolf decided to come around? And where was Uncle Abner, anyway? He wouldn't get far with his cough.

Mr. Tucker must a read my mind. "You sure your uncle has gone home?" he asked.

I shrugged. "Looks like it."

Timothy set himself down on the stump. "We'll wait here until they come back," he said.

My mind scrambled around, trying to figure what to do. If Uncle Abner did git home, they'd catch him for sure. I didn't want to be here then. I looked at Mr. Tucker. "I guess I'll follow you," I said.

He nodded, took a half-burnt stick from the fire, and looked at me. "Can your ma or pa read?"

"Ma can."

So Mr. Tucker scratched a message for her on the stump, right by the Betty lamp. I recognized my name; Ma did teach me that much.

"'Hiram is with me.' That's what I wrote. And I signed my name," Mr. Tucker told me, pointing at the letters. "Come along. You can keep Daniel and Rhoda company."

So that's how I come to be following a crowd of strange men down the hill in the dusk, dragging my feet and wishing I was anywhere else in the world.

25. Daniel

It all happened so fast—one minute, I was hailing Father at the wigwam, telling him I'd found Hobnail Boots. Next instant, he'd gone off with Grandfather and the Ellis men to Hiram's and Mother had hurried away to help Mrs. Ellis's niece, leaving Rhoda and me to wait in the front chamber.

"Keep Jody outside," Father told me. "She'll warn you if

anyone comes. Pull the latchstring in, and don't open the door."

Now Rhoda was asleep behind the curtain, in Mother and Father's bed. The tow lamp sputtered on the hearth and I nearly snuffed it out. I didn't favor the ghostly shadows crawling up the walls, but the light was fast disappearing outside.

My belly growled, asking for food. I picked an apple from the bowl on the table, then set it down. I couldn't eat. I paced the front chamber, though my legs were sore from my dash through the woods. My wampum belt lay on the mantel. I hefted it in my hands, feeling the weight. Grandfather had said it would give me power. Could it protect me from Hobnail Boots? I wrapped it around my waist, cinched it tight. I wished for a looking glass, so I could see myself, but Father always said we'd not enough hard chink for such luxuries.

Jody barked. What now? I hurried to the window and pressed my face to the glass. Torches flickered above dark figures near our gate. Had they come to burn us out? Then Father's voice hailed me. I pulled the latchstring and whispered an oath when I saw a yellow patch of hair behind the four men.

Not again! Gander Head was like the fleas in my bed: always after me. I went into the cold. Father gave his torch to Mr. Ellis and came to me.

"Where's Rhoda?" he asked.

"Asleep." I kept my voice low. "Why is Hiram here?"

"His parents are gone, no sign of them anywhere. No fire on the hearth, no ox or wagon—we durst not leave him alone." Father beckoned and Gander Head shuffled over. "Can you boys behave if we leave you here together?"

Not likely! Of course, I didn't say so.

Hiram scraped a muddy circle in the foreyard with his boot, then looked at Father. "What will you do with my uncle?" he asked.

Uncle? Was Hobnail Boots an uncle to Hiram? I clenched my jaw.

"We'll warn him out of town, if he's the one did the damage," Mr. Ellis said.

"Warn him out? What does that mean?" Hiram asked.

"Just how it sounds." Timothy Ellis came up under the torchlight. "We'll send him down the road. Warn him there's trouble if he comes back."

"But he has a bad cough," Hiram said. "And you don't know he broke up the wigwam."

"Then 'tis true!" I said. "The man I found in the woodlot carried a hatchet. He almost cut me with it, but I kicked it from his hand. He had a fit of coughing, too. Your uncle and the ugly man in the clearing are one and the same."

"Daniel." Father laid a hand on my arm.

Hiram shot me a fierce look. "Every man has a hatchet," he said. "What of it?"

"Someone cut the wigwam apart," I said.

"Come along," Mr. Ellis said. "Time's fleeting."

Father drew close to Grandfather. "Perhaps you should stay with the boys."

"No." Grandfather moved into the circle of light. "I must

go with you. I can match the man's gait with the tracks he left behind." His eyes fastened on my waist and the wampum belt. He stepped close and spoke quietly in Pequot, gesturing with his hands. I puzzled over the words till I understood: I should use the war club, hidden in his chamber, if there was trouble.

"Wegun," I replied.

"Don't use that funny talk," Hiram said.

"Watch the fire," Father said, and he followed the torches toward the road. I shut the door, closing Jody outside, and pulled in the latchstring. Hiram slumped on the bench near the hearth. Our eyes didn't meet.

"'Twas your uncle came after me," I said.

Hiram shrugged. "You got no proof."

I moved close, keeping after him. "He was captured in the raid, wasn't he?"

"So what if he was? That's naught to do with the wigwam. The Injuns kidnapped me, too, but I got loose."

I stared. "You? I thought—" I stared at him. "I thought you hailed from Connecticut."

"We do now." He studied the fire. "But two years back, when the raiders came, we had started a farm down to Royalton, with my uncle. Injuns burnt our house, kilt our cattle, carried Uncle Abner off to Canada. Ma hid in the privy, or she might a been kidnapped, too. We went to my aunt in Connecticut, to wait for the war to end."

Hiram was in the raid? How could that be? My thoughts twisted themselves into a ball as I tried to piece things together. Had we heard the same screams, run from the same musket shots, feared the same butchery?

The backlog popped, sending sparks across the hearth. I took up the twig broom, swept the coals back into the fire, then added another small log, keeping my back to Hiram as flames licked the dry maple. Should I tell him? I took a deep breath.

"The raid came here, too," I said. "Mother and Rhoda and I hid all night in a cave."

"What?" Gander Head's good eye peered at me, his face twisted and strange, as if he couldn't see me right. "But why'd *you* have to hide from the raid? You're Injuns—Indians, I mean. Like the ones what took Abner."

"Mother's people are Pequot," I said. "We're no relation to the men who came with the British. Father was with the Colonials himself, even though he didn't fight."

"That militia waited too late," Hiram said. "They were cowards, Pa says."

I whirled around, making fists. "You can't say that. Father went with them. He was ready to chase them, but the commander made them wait till daylight. Was *your* pa running after them?"

"Naw." Now Hiram looked ashamed. "Pa was trying to save our house, but it weren't no use. It burnt to the ground. We had nothing left but Uncle Abner's ox."

A long howling sounded from the hilltop.

"Wolves!" Hiram cried. "We heard them on the ridge last night."

"No, it's Jody." I ran to the window. "She's up at the broken wigwam." I put my face to the glass, but my own rippled reflection stared back. Jody's howl turned to the bark that told us a stranger was near—and then her cry came on strange, almost frantic. "She's hurt." I pulled on my coat and found my hat.

"Where you going?" Hiram asked.

"To get Jody. You stay and listen for Rhoda."

"Why? She ain't *my* sister."

I peeked around the curtain. Rhoda slept soundly. Jody howled again, then yipped and keened. Had Hiram's uncle caught my dog? I pushed the logs to the back of the fire with the poker, then ducked into Grandfather's chamber and felt in the dark for the war club, hidden beneath the folds of the wolf skin. I hoisted it to my chest. The smooth chestnut was heavy with the power of its *mundtu*.

"What's that thing?" Hiram asked.

"Grandfather's war club." I held it up to the firelight, where it gleamed as if it had its own fire inside. I touched the belt at my waist. I was as strong as I could ever be.

26. Hiram

"Wait for me!" I yelled, but Daniel lit out ahead of me. I couldn't hardly see a thing, what with the dark and my eye half shut. I stumbled after him.

The dog howled and carried on as we got close. My good

eye got used to the dark when we hit the top of the hill, and I caught up to Daniel. The dog was caught in twine under a sapling, all twisted up like she was in a fishnet. Daniel cut her loose with his knife and she jumped all over him.

"Uncle Abner?" I called, and I was glad when he didn't answer. He'd come on so mean, I didn't hardly know him.

We looked around but didn't see nobody. The dog chased around the wigwam twice, snuffling at the ground. Then she took off through the wheat field, loping acrost the stubble. We followed after her, running fast as we could.

The dog circled to the bottom of the field. I tripped and fell twice in the ruts. In the starlight I seen Daniel drop his club, then stoop to pick it up. He grunted. It must a been heavy, but he didn't complain. Jody led us out to the road, then back up their trail. Daniel opened the gate and we kept running toward his house.

Suddenly, the dog stopped. She was barking and snarling and carrying on. "Ouch!" I rapped my shins on that door that stood open by that hole in the ground, the one Pa said was a cellar.

"Hiram?" Coughing come up from the hole and then two hands grabbed the edge. I smelled my uncle's rank, cold sweat.

"Uncle Abner!" I yelled. "What are you doing down there?"

"What's it look like?" He reached his hand up to me, but I didn't take it. "I fell in. The ladder's broke. Help me out."

He grabbed for my foot. I jumped back and Daniel

slammed his club right on my uncle's fingers. I don't know who howled louder, Abner or the dog.

"Shut the doors!" Daniel yelled.

I didn't even think, just grabbed my side of the trap door, pushed hard, and let go. *Thud!* Mine fell. *Thud!* There went the other one. I didn't want to look. Was Uncle Abner's fingers smashed?

Daniel shoved me. "Sit down!" We plunked ourselves on the lid. Uncle Abner pushed and hammered underneath us, hollering words Ma would a whupped me for. Jody growled and snarled. The door of the house opened and Rhoda stood there screaming. A white petticoat whipped around her legs.

"Rhoda, stay there!" Daniel told her.

"Open up!" Uncle Abner yelled. He started in coughing again.

We held on tight, laying ourselves across the doors. "He can't breathe!" I said.

"Yes he can," Daniel said. "I hide in there sometimes."

"He'll kill us for sure if he gets out," I said.

The doors buckled and bumped under us. Uncle Abner must have heaved them with his shoulder, sick as he was. Just when I thought we'd have to give up, I seen torchlight down by the road.

"Here come the men," I said.

"Father! Grandfather!" Daniel yelled. "He's here! We caught him!"

They had a crowd this time: Mr. Tucker and the old man; Daniel's ma; the Ellis men; that Mr. Durkee, who brought

Uncle Abner the other night—they was all running. The torches sent sparks into the sky like lightning bugs. And there was someone else, too—Pa.

I forgot about Uncle Abner, forgot about holding the door, forgot about the whupping I was owed. I run to Pa and tucked myself under his arm as he gripped my shoulders.

"What happened?" he asked.

"Uncle Abner's trapped in their cellar. Where you been? I thought you'd left me."

"Don't be foolish. We went to see about a place for our store," Pa said. "Now hush. We've enough trouble on our hands."

We watched while the men hauled Uncle Abner out. He hissed and growled at them like a bobcat and Daniel's dog snapped at him. The men held the torches high to light Uncle Abner's face. Mr. Ellis, the older one, took my uncle's arms and held them behind his back. Daniel's ma lifted her skirts and run to Rhoda. She wrapped her in a shawl and scooped her up.

"Let go of me!" Uncle Abner tried to twist away. Then he spots Daniel's grandpa. He reared his head back like an angry mule, screwed up his face, and spat a nasty wad at the old man.

I ain't going to say the words they shouted then. Some I never heard before. It was a ruckus, with everyone yelling, the dog barking, Rhoda crying, and Pa yelling, "Abner, don't be a fool! He had nothing to do with the raid."

Then my uncle starts in to coughing until he's doubled

over, and Mr. Ellis eased up, letting him slump to his knees. Daniel's ma pushed into the circle.

"Caleb, leave him be," she said. "Let him catch his breath."

Soon as Miz Tucker opened her mouth, everyone got quiet. How did she do that? The men stepped aside while Abner coughed something awful.

"All right." Timothy Ellis spoke up now. "If he's the man who wrecked the wigwam, let's warn him out of town."

I looked up at Pa, waiting for him to say something, but he kept his mouth pressed in a tight line.

The Injun chief said some of those strange-sounding words and Daniel's ma starts in talking. "My father says our way is to hold a council with our sachem. We would decide, together, what to do with him. But we have no sachem here."

A sachem? What was that? I wanted to ask Pa, but he was all torn up, his mouth twisting and his fists clenched tight like it was his brother that done wrong, not Ma's.

Uncle Abner stopped coughing and stood up slow, looking all around. His eyes was a funny orange color in the torchlight, like a pumpkin. I shivered when those eyes landed on me. "What's all the fuss about?" Uncle Abner asked. He coughed again. "I'm sorry I fell into your cellar— I didn't see the door open in the dark. That young half-breed nearly broke my fingers with his club, like a wild savage. Guess we know where that comes from." He gives Daniel a nasty look, then his ma.

"You're the savage!" Mr. Tucker jumped at him, his hands going right for my uncle's neck.

"Hold on!" Timothy Ellis grabbed Mr. Tucker. Mr. Ellis and Mr. Durkee dragged Uncle Abner backward. Pinned his arms like they meant to tie them in a knot.

"Enough!" Mr. Ellis yelled. "My niece would be in the ground if it weren't for Miz Tucker's physicks the last two days. We know what needs doing. Let's get on with it. We'll send him downriver where he belongs."

Uncle Abner twisted and squirmed. "Do what you want," he said. "But I didn't do nothing to your dirty wigwam." He pointed at me. "Ask Hiram who broke it down. He's been sneaking over here every chance he gets."

"That's a lie!" I yelled. "It was wrecked when I saw it."

Now the torches was held up over me. I squinched up my good eye and threw my arm acrost my face. The sounds started up: hoofbeats clattering along the river, cows bawling, that hawk screaming right over my head—

And then, something else. Daniel's voice.

"Hiram didn't do it."

My mouth opened so wide, a bat could a flown in.

Daniel stepped right into that torchlight circle beside me, but his eyes was on his grandfather.

"Daniel's right." Rhoda took my hand. "Hiram didn't break up the wigwam." A few days ago, I would a pushed her away. Now I held on to those cold fingers.

Rhoda turned to face all those men. She was brave. "Hiram helped us build it," she told them.

Uncle Abner sneered and looked around the circle a men. "You believe them? Dirty half-breeds?"

Daniel pointed to Uncle Abner's boots, the ones he'd borrowed from Pa. "You left your tracks all over," Daniel said. "Hobnail boot tracks."

Tracks! Now that was smart. Why didn't I think of that?

Uncle Abner squirmed like a cornered rabbit, but he couldn't get away.

"Let's take him to my place," Mr. Durkee said. "We'll stand watch tonight and warn him off in the morning."

"Wait." Pa finally opened his mouth. He reached into his pocket, pulled out some bills and coins, and stepped over to Uncle Abner. "What you done was wrong," he said. "I won't argue with these men. Take this currency, small as it is. Hannah will never forgive me if I send you off without a single penny. Go home to the rest of the family, in Connecticut. They'll nurse you back to health."

My uncle's face was near purple in the torchlight. "You don't know enough to lap salt," he told Pa, "staying in this godforsaken place. You can rot with Satan for all I care."

"Enough of your foul talk," Mr. Ellis said. "There are women and children here. Come along."

The men circled around my uncle and pushed him along in the dark. Daniel's ma was telling Mr. Durkee what to give Uncle Abner for his cough, and Pa was saying something to me, but I didn't listen. I was watching Daniel, finding his face when a torch passed by and lit it up. Just staring at him.

He stared right back.

Part IV

ɞɞɞ

Flying West

27. Daniel

The front chamber was cold and dark. I raked the coals, gave them my breath, fed them strips of birch bark, kindling, small logs. The flames blazed up. Rhoda curled on the bench, wrapped in Mother's shawl. Making the fire kept my mind busy, but fear gnawed at me, like *A'waumps* chewing his way out of a trap.

I'd left my sister alone. I would be punished.

Mother lit the tow lamp. Her silence was dark. Did she know what I had done?

Grandfather came in, carrying the war club, and I stood to face him. "I'm sorry," I said. "I forgot."

"The club is not all you forgot." Mother's voice, once soft as water trickling, was hard now. I wished I were in the loft, hidden under my blankets. Wished I had never left the cave in the hemlock ravine. Wished—

Rhoda sat up straight and threw off her shawl. "You left me alone. I was scared." Her eyes were big and staring, as they had been after her dream. "I heard the man yelling in the cellar. The tow lamp was out. I called, but no one came. You shouldn't do that."

"I know." I sat beside her and tried to pull her close, but she twisted away. "I'm sorry. You were asleep, and I thought Hiram's uncle was hurting Jody up at the wigwam."

"Tell us what happened," Mother said.

No use tarrying, so I told them how Jody howled, then cried in pain. How I ran to rescue her. How she led us across the mowing ground and around to the cellar.

"Hiram's uncle broke the ladder when he fell in," I said. "I hit his hands with Grandfather's club and we trapped him inside." I stood tall for a moment. Perhaps 'twas wrong, but I felt a strange pride, thinking how the club's *mundtu* helped me strike the ugly man's hands.

Grandfather stepped close to Mother. "Daughter, I bade him take up the club to protect himself."

Mother's eyes made black coals. "He left Rhoda alone."

How could I explain Jody's mournful cries? "I'm sorry. I didn't think." In truth, I should have cared for my sister, not my dog. Shame prickled all over me.

The cold night rushed in with Father, who stomped his feet and strode over to me, Jody at his heels. I felt even smaller beneath his gaze. "Daniel," he said. "You're lucky no harm came to Rhoda."

"Yes sir." I lowered my eyes and reached for Jody, but she slipped past me, settling by the fire. Even my dog had turned her back on me!

Mother spoke to Grandfather in Pequot and he nodded.

"Tomorrow, I will share lessons with Daniel, to help him find a better way," Grandfather said.

Father dropped his hat on the table. He loosened his hair, combed it with his long fingers, sat on the stump beside the fire. "What kind of 'lessons' can teach a boy to obey his father?" he asked.

"He needs to return to the right path," Grandfather said.

Father's scar showed his fury. "That is all very well. But please, allow me to discipline my son."

I squirmed on the bench as if a nest of snakes had crawled up my breeches. What was the right path? Would Grandfather send me alone into the forest, to wait for dreams and visions? My heart stormed in my chest. I wished to climb onto the back of Rhoda's hawk and fly toward the stars until I heard naught but the wind and the sound of the hawk's wings, beating and beating—

"Father, what's wrong?"

Mother jumped to her feet and gripped Grandfather's arms. I plummeted down from my dream as Grandfather's face froze, his eyes blinked fast—too fast!—and his mouth moved. No words came out, only strange, broken sounds, and spittle. Rhoda screamed and Father lunged to catch Grandfather before he fell.

"'Tis a fit," Father said. "Quick, sit him down. Daniel, help us."

We guided Grandfather to the bench and wrapped him tight with Mother's shawl. Rhoda ran for the wolf skin and laid it across his lap. I fetched a cup of water and held it to his lips, but he couldn't swallow.

Soon as it began, it was over. Grandfather's spirit came back into his eyes. He looked from one of us to another. "What happened?" he asked. His words were slurred.

"You are fatigued from this long day," Mother said. Lines of worry pulled at her mouth.

"I spoke too harshly," Father said. "I'm sorry. We'll help you to bed. Can you stand?" He and Mother lifted Grandfather gently to his feet.

Grandfather seemed small and old as they led him away on unsteady legs.

"Does he need medicine?" Rhoda called after them.

They didn't answer. Rhoda and I looked at each other, then climbed to our pallets without speaking. I found Rhoda's hand, and we held on tight until sleep swept over us.

In the morning, I found that Father and Grandfather had already settled on my punishment. I would spend half of each day with Grandfather, rebuilding the wigwam, the other half working with Father. At candle lighting, I would practice my letters and numbers. "You are not to leave our sides for any reason," Father said.

I kept my eyes on the ground. This seemed no different from a usual day, filled with chores. Where was the punishment?

There were no words about Grandfather's sudden fit. He

seemed himself, though a bit unsteady, and he linked his arm through Mother's as we climbed the hill.

It took us most of the forenoon to rebuild the wigwam. Timothy Ellis came to help and the work went fast. First we lashed the poles together for the frame; then Rhoda and I gathered the shingles and held them up for Father and Timothy, who layered them one atop the other. Mother cut and threaded the new twine while Grandfather and I pinned the shingles together. The sides grew quickly, then the rounded roof with its smoke hole at the top. For once, no Hiram— yet it felt strange, building the wigwam without him. Was he being punished, too?

Timothy Ellis stood back with his hands on his hips. "A whole house built in a morning," he said. "No post-and-beam or log home ever rose so fast." He peered inside. "'Tis snug," he said. "I might try one myself, next time we feel the pinch at our farm."

Rhoda ducked inside and poked her head out at us. "Can we make a fire?" she asked.

"Yes," Grandfather said. "We'll gather the wood now."

"I can help," I said, but Grandfather shook his head. "Your lessons are over for today."

Rhoda whispered in my ear as I slipped from the wigwam. "Maybe you can stay longer tomorrow," she said.

At least Rhoda bore me no malice. Yet my heart was torn as I followed Father down the hill. He and Grandfather had split me down the middle. Rhoda would be first to light a fire in the wigwam, first to help Grandfather unpack his things. Since her dream, Grandfather treated Rhoda with new respect, and my feelings on this darted back and forth, like a honeybee flitting from one flower to another. I was glad Grandfather no longer spoke to me of being a *powwaw*. But did he think I was not worthy? Had he chosen Rhoda instead?

Father set me to the worst chore on the farm: cleaning dung from the barn. Then, after I'd hauled it to the dung heap, he bade me hitch the oxen. Old Red was frisky in the cold, but Father raised no hand to help me. He gave me the reins and I drove the oxen to the smithy to pick up our wagon. Father walked behind me. His silence stung more than the stinking work of cleaning the stable.

Mr. Chase helped me back the team up to the wagon hitch. "Mr. Durkee tells me you had a ruckus at your place last night," he said to Father.

"We warned a man out of town." Father's voice was calm, as though this happened every day in Griswold. "He broke up the old man's home, caused us considerable distress. We can't allow that."

"Didn't I warn you there'd be trouble with those prisoners?" Mr. Chase said.

"Aye," said Father. "But this one escaped before the release. I trust you'll let us know if you ever see the man here again—and spread the word to our other neighbors." He told of Abner's lame leg, his cough, his burnt red hair. Then Father startled me. "We mean no harm to the Coombs family," he said. "We know they will be good neighbors."

Hiram's family—good neighbors? Had Father gone as buffle brained as Hiram? I rubbed Jemmy's nose to cover my surprise.

It was near dusk when we headed home. The wind crept up my back and into my sleeves. Winter was coming on. I thought on the canoe I hoped to make with Grandfather. Would we have to wait until spring? Perhaps he had forgotten. I felt empty as the trees above me, stripped of their last leaves by the storm.

Next day, the wind's bluster kept us inside. Father set me to chores in the forenoon while Mother straightened the mess Hiram's uncle had left in the root cellar. Rhoda skipped off to the wigwam with Grandfather, holding his hand. I whittled pegs for the mare's bridle with my new knife, fixed the pegs to the wall, then helped Father repair the sheep pen. My hands were happy, working with knife and hammer, and I tucked away a smile. Making things was punishment for Father, but not for me. Still, when sounds of hammering drifted from the wigwam, it seemed unfair. If only I had a twin and could be in both places at once!

Grandfather waited for my lessons till candle lighting, when Rhoda and I carried a basket of food to the wigwam. We ducked under an old blanket serving for a door. Grandfather had laid a fire inside a circle of flat stones. Smoke took its time finding the hole in the roof, and made my eyes smart.

Grandfather sat cross-legged on a sleeping platform, the black wolf skin beneath him. He was dressed as he had been on his first night, with the copper pendant on his bare chest. "Welcome," Grandfather said. "Sit down."

Rhoda and I sat beside the fire and took the cloth from the basket while Grandfather waited in silence. Firelight lit the tail of the fox quiver. Grandfather's clothes hung from a cedar pole and his other bundles made shadowy lumps beneath the sleeping platform. This was his home now.

Though Mother's food was fragrant, I did not eat. Grandfather smiled at me through the smoke. "Did the story of *Chahnameed* steal your appetite?" he asked.

I shook my head. "What lesson do you have for me?"

"Some might call these stories or tales," Grandfather said. "They are not like the lessons your father gives you at night. *My* grandfather, who was Mohegan, gave them to me." He parted the smoke with his hand as it curled up between us. "Perhaps your mother has told you that Pequots and Mohegans have long been both friends and enemies. We also married into each other's families. You have Mohegan as well as Pequot blood, and our language is almost the same."

Mohegan blood, *Owamux*—what next? My blood flowed the same red as Father's, as Mother's or Grandfather's. Who could tell what drop belonged where? Would I always be trying to sort through this mix, leaning toward the Pequot side one minute, *Owamux* the next?

Grandfather rubbed his eyes. "Come where I can see you," he said. "You are too far away."

How could he not see us? He sat as close as the length of our arms. Still, Rhoda and I joined Grandfather on the wolf skin and he began to speak, first telling of *Cautantowwit,* our creator. "He gave us a world of order, of balance and harmony," Grandfather said, and told us how the earth's four directions direct the traveler and call the winds to us.

"When the wind whistles from the east, we must take care," Grandfather said. "It can be a bad omen." I glanced at Rhoda, thinking on her whistling dream, but her eyes were fastened to Grandfather's face. A chill slid up my back. Had her dream foretold the fury of Hiram's uncle?

Grandfather kept talking. He spoke of the good things that have come from the west and southwest, such as corn and beans, brought to us by the crow many years ago. He told how Father Sun rides on the back of *Doyup,* Grandfather Turtle, as he rises and falls each day. How the hawk and the eagle fly higher than all other birds. "They carry our prayers to the Creator," Grandfather said.

"Like Rhoda's hawk?" I asked.

Grandfather nodded. His lessons swam between Pequot and English, the two tongues tangled so that I heard each story in pieces.

The warmth of the fire made my eyes heavy. Rhoda slumped against me, her head in my lap. Grandfather nudged me awake.

"Your lesson is not over," he said softly. "I must speak of the Beautiful Path." He took his tobacco pouch from his belt and pulled a clay pipe from beneath his pallet.

"Where is the pouch your mother made for you?" he asked.

I lowered my eyes. "I don't know."

Grandfather sighed. "You must find it. You will need it to carry your most precious things, and for tobacco." He tamped the fragrant leaves into the bowl of his pipe, lit it, and took a deep breath, then let the smoke out slowly. "This smoke will float up to the Smokey Way in the sky," Grandfather said.

"Father calls it the Milky Way," Rhoda said, and struggled to sit up, rubbing her eyes. I pulled her close for both warmth and comfort.

"We must walk on the Beautiful Path as we travel from this life to the next," Grandfather said. He sucked on the pipe again, then released his breath. "Like Father Sun, we are born in the east. We follow him to the west when we die."

"But the sun comes back in the morning," Rhoda murmured.

"Yes," Grandfather said. "His trail is a circle." He smoked again. "We can send smoke to the Smokey Way above us, to those who have already followed the path west." He blew a long plume of smoke from his mouth. The tobacco smoke mingled with smoke from the fire and drifted through the hole toward the night sky.

"My grandfather taught me that some stars burn more brightly with the souls of those who have passed into the spirit world," Grandfather said. "You can look for them tonight, when the stars come out." He passed me the pipe. "Your turn."

My hands shook, but not from the heat of the pipe's bowl. Why was Grandfather giving me a lesson about death? "Father forbids me to use tobacco," I said.

"Yes," Grandfather said. "The pipe is only for special times."

I hesitated. Should I obey Father, or Grandfather? Once again, I felt like the seam on a sleeve, rent down the middle.

"If I smoke the tobacco, does that mean I must become a *powwaw?*" I asked.

Grandfather shook his head. "No. You will find your own way."

He spoke in riddles. "What about Rhoda? Can a girl be a *powwaw?*"

"It happened sometimes, in the past, but the old ways are gone now. She has a healer's hands. *Your* hands may help you follow another path."

Whatever my hands might do, they were too warm now. I sucked on the pipe stem and bitter smoke filled my lungs, making me cough. Grandfather pounded my back and took the pipe. He tapped the last of the tobacco into the fire, then dipped a cup into his water bucket and set it to my lips. The cool water soothed my throat, and I rubbed tears from my eyes.

"Lessons are over for tonight," Grandfather said. "Remember my words."

"We will," Rhoda said. "Thank you, Grandfather."

We stumbled outside. The stars glittered above us. Grandfather didn't expect me to be a *powwaw.* Then what was my path? And how would I find it? I felt buffeted by a wind that came at me from every direction, even though the night was still.

I tried to study my hands, but it was too dark to see them. I knew my fingers were long and thin, the nails broken and cracked from hard work. Where would they take me?

Rhoda's hand slid into mine and I looked down on her. Grandfather's words didn't puzzle her, or make her fret. Was she too young—or just wiser than everyone else?

"Which stars are the brightest?" Rhoda asked.

"I don't know." Some blazed, then faded when a wisp of cloud passed over them. Others pulsed with a cold, quiet light. I turned my face to the current of stars, splattered across the sky. Father called it the Milky Way. To Grandfather, it was the Smokey Way. To me, it was like the White River twisting through our valley. Which name held the truth?

28. Daniel

"Eat your breakfast," Father said the next morning. "We have an errand to do."

I was slow with my porridge, thinking perhaps he planned a trip to the gristmill, where the men talked for hours while heavy millstones ground our wheat to flour. Instead, we cut through the meadow ground, walked down the hill to the river, and crossed a narrow bridge.

Water trickled around the rocks: too shallow for a canoe or for fishing. I sighed and caught up with Father. The path wound through alders and opened into a clearing holding a rough cabin and a long, low shed. Father waved me over and rapped on the door.

"Come in!" a voice called.

The sweet smell of new wood tickled my nose as we stepped inside. A man stood up from a stool by the window. He was tall, with a smooth face. His black hair, longer than mine, was pulled back in a knot. Sawdust and shavings flecked his leather apron.

"David Sykes," the man said. "Good day to you."

"Caleb Tucker," Father said. They shook hands. "My son, Daniel."

"Pleased to meet you, young man." Mr. Sykes took my hand as if I were already grown. "Look around, if you'd like," he told me.

I wandered the room while he talked to Father, my eyes touching everything: Drawknives of every shape and size. Planks of smooth ash and maple. Strange tools I had never seen, hanging from the rafters. In one corner, wooden staves leaning against each other. In another, iron hoops of every shape and size—

"Oh!" I turned to him. "You're the new cooper," I said.

"Aye. And busy, as you can see," he said.

Father went out back in search of a barrel. Mr. Sykes set an unfinished barrel on a stump and tipped it to bring one open end to his waist. He held up a sharp blade with a lip and two handles, almost like a razor. "It's a draw shave," he told me, and drew it away, shearing thin slivers of wood from a stave. "Like shaving a man's face."

The barrel wobbled. Without thinking, my hand went out to steady it.

"Good lad," he said. He turned the barrel slowly, running his hand over each stave, and set it down. "Feel the rim."

My hand followed the path he'd made with his own. One stave didn't match the rest. "This one is too tall."

"Right. Fetch me the chamfer knife and we'll fix it."

He pointed to a flat, square knife with a handle on each end. He drew it across the rim with a few swift strokes. "Take a turn?" he asked.

"I don't know how. My knife is different."

"You won't learn unless you try." He set the chamfer knife in my hand.

I looked up. His eyes, the color of dark tea, met mine. I drew the knife to me, but it caught and made a gouge. "Let me show you." Mr. Sykes tilted my hands to a different angle. This time, I shaved only a thin curl of wood, as if I were working on Rhoda's doll.

"Put him to work, did you?" Father had come back, holding a small barrel to his chest.

"Your son has a calling," Mr. Sykes said.

I smiled, though I knew I shouldn't take pride in a compliment.

"He's good with his hands," Father said. "I prefer driving the goose quill myself."

"Let him visit me sometimes," the cooper said. "Would you like that, Daniel?"

"Yes *sir*," I said. I felt warm to my toes, as if I'd eaten two bowls of Mother's rabbit stew.

Father and Mr. Sykes agreed to trade wheat seed for the barrel. "My wife is skilled at making physics," Father said, "though I hope you won't need them."

"Ah." Mr. Sykes smiled at me. "So your mother must be the Indian doctress I have heard about. We have blood in common."

Blood. There was that word again. "But how——"

"My grandmother was Abenaki," Mr. Sykes said. "She married a Frenchman. And you are——"

"Pequot," I told him. "And a little bit Mohegan," I added.

Father's bushy eyebrow arched toward his scar. "Since when?" he asked. "You are part English, too. Or have you forgotten?"

"No, Father," I said, and blushed. "But you said we are all Americans now."

"True enough." Father laughed. "You listen well."

Mr. Sykes set a hand on my shoulder. "Never mind who's who. Tell me, if you could build anything, what would it be?"

Once again, the words spilled out before I could stop them. "I want to make a dugout canoe with my grandfather."

Father rubbed his beard. "More surprises," he said, but he smiled this time.

"That's hard work," Mr. Sykes said. "You'd best get at it before winter comes." He shook hands with Father, then with me. "Come back soon," he told me.

I glanced at Father. "May I?"

"I expect so," he said.

Not quite yes, but near enough. I took one last look around the shop, and the cooper waved. I smiled and waved back before following Father to the bridge. He was quiet, his brow wrinkled.

"I think the lessons were meant for me today," Father said. He slapped my back. "Go along now. Your punishment is over."

29. Hiram

Ma weren't fit to live with after they warned Uncle Abner out of town. She stormed around the house like a cat dropped in water, hissing and scratching. "You're a coward, with no backbone," she told Pa. "How could you drive my own flesh and blood away, when he was so sick?" Pa didn't say nothing, just hung his head.

And me? She said I was a sneak, an Injun lover who betrayed my own uncle. If I went next door again, she'd have my hide.

Course, I knew she'd never catch me, not with her belly so big she bumped into everything. She hardly fit through the front door. I wanted to run back to Daniel's, see what happened with the wigwam. And I wondered: Was Daniel in trouble, too?

That first morning, Pa hauled me off to the woods as if he might whup me—but he never did, just give me a scolding about running off.

"It's a good thing Abner's gone," Pa said. "The cabin's too small already, with the baby coming. We have to watch our food, make sure we have enough to get through the winter. And that British prison made Abner crazy. I think your ma agrees, but she'll never say so." Pa winked. "Walk careful coming home, like I swatted you some."

That made me grin. Me and Pa was in this together.

Next day, Ma was up before either of us, unpacking barrels like she was finally ready to move in. She set Pa and me to work. We patched the roof, then brought in wood, fixed the big iron hook over the fire for her kettle, built a platform for their bed, and made a shelf for her plates and spoons. She was right behind us, stitching a curtain to hide the pallet, setting plates and toddy mugs on the new shelf. Soon as we finished one chore, she thought of another one.

"Take it easy, Hannah," Pa said, but she paid him no mind, even though her face was red as the quilt she found in one of the barrels.

"She's like a squirrel, getting her nest ready for the winter," Pa told me.

"Does she have to do it all at once?" I asked. "It ain't winter yet."

Ma went on like this for days, till one night, I was so

worn out I fell asleep with all my clothes on, sprawled across the stump. I dreamt of a tomcat moaning and woke up hearing Ma carrying on behind the curtain. It weren't even first light, but Pa was stoking up the fire.

"What's wrong?" I asked him.

"The baby is coming a mite too soon," Pa said. "Run to Miz Durkee, at the gristmill."

Gray light barely showed above the trees. It was a long way to the mill. Time I got back with Miz Durkee, Ma's screams carried all the way to the road. Pa wouldn't let me in, but he wouldn't let me leave, neither. He sent me for wood, then water, then wood again.

All at once, Ma screamed like the women in the Injun raid. I dropped my bundle of logs and run to the door, scared my own bad sounds would catch me.

Pa grabbed ahold a me. His face was as gray as the sky. "The baby's here," he said. "Something's wrong. It ain't breathing right and your ma—" Pa's face crumpled up. He was crying! "Run to Miz Tucker."

"But Ma said—"

"I don't care," Pa said. "She'll die if we don't get help quick. Run!"

So I did. Frost made the grass slick. I slipped twice but kept going, over the brook, acrost the wheat field, through the fence. I was yelling soon as I could see the house, yelling so loud I didn't watch where I was going. I come around the barn and smashed hard, right into Daniel.

"Watch out!" he yelled.

We got tangled in a pile. I scrambled up, still yelling. "Miz Tucker! Help!"

Doors opened and everyone come running. Rhoda, Miz Tucker, even the old man, Daniel and his pa, they all stared at me. I couldn't talk right.

"Ma," I said. "Baby. Ma——"

"Calm down, Yellow Hair." The old man took hold a me.

"Take a breath," Miz Tucker said.

I gulped for air, tried again. "The baby——come out. Pa says it won't breathe right. And he says Ma might die." I clutched my belly. "Ma don't want you there, but Pa told me——"

"Hiram, be still." That Miz Tucker, she sure can make you do things. I clamped my mouth shut.

"Go to Mrs. Ellis next door," Miz Tucker said. "Ask her to gather the women and come to your place."

I bit my lip. "Those Ellis men don't like me on account of Uncle Abner."

"Nonsense," Miz Tucker said, but she told Daniel to go with me. "Hurry," she said.

We was already running. Daniel took off ahead a me and I pushed to keep up. We ran flat-out down the grass track, acrost a cornfield, and up to a big house. Something was thumping and bumping inside. Daniel banged on the door like he'd been here before and hurried in when someone called to us.

The chamber was full of women. A short, fat one walked back and forth in front of a big spinning wheel. The thumping noise came from the loom, where a woman was weaving. Another one sat by the fire, combing wool. I tried to find my voice again.

"My ma—"

Daniel helped me. "Mother says can you come to Mrs. Coombs, to help with her baby," he said. "And bring the other women if you can."

"Ma might die," I told them.

"Don't fret," the big woman said. "Kate has firm hands. You boys go on home. Martha and I will be along as fast as we can."

We run back to Daniel's. I heard hoofbeats and Daniel's ma galloped past on that bony old mare. Her braids was flying out behind her. She didn't even have a saddle, and she carried a big basket over one arm. Her skirts was up to her knees and I seen her petticoats. My neck felt hot. I thought of all the bad things Ma and Uncle Abner and me had said about Injuns. What would Ma do, when she seen an Injun woman in her chamber? Would it scare her to death?

"Can your ma save mine?" I asked Daniel.

"I don't know," he said.

Daniel looked after his ma until we couldn't see her no more. Finally, he turned around, shaking. He was as skairt as I was.

Mr. Tucker come out a their barn and we rushed over to him. "That Miz Ellis said she'd come, and her daughter, too." I bent down, trying to catch my breath. "I'd best go home."

"Not now," Mr. Tucker said. "Stay awhile. You'll be fine

with Rhoda and Daniel, up at the wigwam. I'll go to your place to be certain everything is all right." He gives Daniel a sharp look from under his hat. "Do as your grandfather says." He was hurrying through the gate and acrost the cornfield afore either one of us could speak a word.

Daniel didn't seem too keen on being with me. He went up the hill without saying boo and I followed along. Truth is, I weren't too partial on going home, not with Ma carrying on. Besides, I hadn't seen the wigwam since they'd built it back up.

Smoke was coming out the hole at the top. We ducked in under a blanket. The old man was inside, setting on a platform with Rhoda. I tarried a minute until I could see through the smoke. Rhoda and the old man was singing a strange song. He crumbled some old dried leaves into a bowl in his lap. It didn't look like nothing I'd want to eat, even with my belly so empty.

Daniel went in to set beside the old chief, but there weren't no room for me. My eyes stung. Must a been the smoke. I went back out, even though my jacket weren't very warm.

"Yellow Hair!" the old man called.

I didn't answer to that insult. He should call me Hiram by now. They kept on with their noise. It weren't much of a song. More like a chant, and a strange one, too. It made my skin prickle.

I picked up stones and tossed them at the stone wall. *Ping. Ping.* I threw pebbles first, then bigger stones. *Thwack! Thump!* Still I heard their voices.

A crow screeched in the tree. *"Caw! Caw!"*

I looked up. Another crow flew into that oak tree. Then another. And another. A whole flock a them, cawing and shrieking, flying around me the way they tease a hawk to scare it off. More crows than I'd ever seen. "Git!" I yelled. I took off my jacket and swung it over my head, but they kept after me, swooping and diving.

I grabbed more stones, hurled them at the birds. "Git outta here!" I missed. All I did was make them madder. And louder.

The old man comes outta the wigwam. His eyes were strange. "Hiram, stop! Do not anger them. They are messengers."

"What do you mean? Crows can't talk." Sometimes, the old man was a fool.

The crows cawed louder. And then, the noises come over me, thumping like hoofbeats coming up the valley. Screaming like women crying for help. Bawling like oxen running from the knife. And me shouting, with my fingers in my ears, "No! Leave me be! Let me go!"

Next thing I knew, the old man had hold of my shoulders. He shook me once, then twice. The noises flew back out a my own head and into the oak tree. They was only crows bickering and jabbering. Daniel and Rhoda stared at me like I was buffle brained.

"What do you hear?" the old man asked.

I fixed my eyes on the ground. "Nothing."

He must a known I was lying. He set his hand under my chin, until I had to look at him. "A demon lives inside you," he said. "But we can chase it away."

"There ain't no demon—it's just—some ugly noises, that's all. I told you, I don't like them crows." I spat at the tree to show him what I meant.

"Didn't you hear me? Don't anger them." The old man kept a tight hold on me, though I tried to twist away. "Listen," he said. "I was a *powwaw* once, a medicine man. I am old; I have lost many of my powers, but demons meddle with Indians and *Owamux* alike. Perhaps I can help you."

"What's *Owamux?*"

"A white person. Someone like you," the old man said. "If you give me something of value, I will try to banish the demons."

I turned my pockets inside out. "I ain't got nothing."

But he weren't looking at me now. A feather come down from the tree and the old man let me loose. Rhoda ran to catch it, but he barked some strange words to keep her back. He wouldn't let Daniel go near it, neither.

"What's wrong?" I asked. "It's just an old crow feather, ain't it?"

I bent to pick it up, but the old man swatted my hand.

"Don't tempt death," he said.

Death? And demons? I swallowed hard. I'd had enough. I danced away from him, run for the wall, and took off for home.

30. Daniel

Hiram ran, but we hardly noticed. For the first time since he'd come to us, Grandfather had fear in his eyes.

"*Kaukont's* feather brings a warning," Grandfather said.

"Why?" Rhoda asked. "You said *Kaukont* brought us corn and beans."

"Yes, but he also carries news from the spirit world," Grandfather said. "Like your dream of the whistling wind."

"What kind of warning?" I asked.

"Death," Grandfather said.

As he spoke, the wind lifted the feather and dropped it near our feet. Rhoda and I jumped back and held each other tight. Grandfather kept his eyes on the feather, as if it were a snake about to strike, while the crows kept whirling and crying. They landed in the oak, then lifted again. Their wings sliced the air, black knives cutting through white smoke. I wanted to stop my ears and run away, like Hiram.

At last, Grandfather spoke. "Daniel, follow Hiram. Find your mother and be sure she is safe in the house of Yellow Hair."

My heart was thumping. Could Mother die? I durst not speak the words. "What should I tell her?"

"Say that crows are flying and a feather has fallen. She will know what to do. Be swift."

My feet wanted to move, but my thoughts kept me back. "Father said we must stay here."

"I will fix it with him later," Grandfather said. "Go." He pulled Rhoda close.

I ran.

I came out of the woods into their clearing and near tripped over Hiram. He sat on a stump, his arms wrapped around his knees.

"What ails you now?" I asked.

He pointed at the cabin. "Listen. There's no sound. Ma must be dead."

My heart battered loud enough to wake the squirrels in their hollow trees. Mrs. Coombs could die—was that *Kaukont's* message? Please, let it be Hiram's mother, not mine—

I stopped myself. I shouldn't wish death on anyone, not even Mrs. Coombs with her talk so full of malice—should I?

Sparks shot from the chimney. An ox nibbled on a tree branch near the house. Was the silence a good omen, or a bad one?

All at once, a wailing scream filled the clearing and brought us to our feet. "Ma!" Hiram yelled, and chased down the path. I went after him. The sharp points of newly cut brush dug into my moccasins. We pulled up at the door, out of breath. Hiram knocked, as if we stood at the house of a stranger. I held my breath. Mrs. Durkee opened the door and squinted at us. A long homespun cloth was draped over her arm.

"What do you boys want?"

I paid her no mind and stepped around her, my eyes searching for Mother. The chamber was dark and I didn't see her, but soon I heard her soothing voice, soft as running water, coming from behind a curtain, and my breath came out in a rush. Things would be fine now.

And then we heard another sound, like a sick kitten mewling.

"That's my baby," Hiram said, and he pushed past me into the chamber.

31. Hiram

The chamber was filled with women. A bad smell hung in the air like smoke. Miz Durkee, the one I'd fetched this morning, held a cloth up to the fire. Martha Ellis, that bony one I'd seen working the loom, had her back to us. Miz Ellis, with the round face, sat in Ma's rocker holding a bundle against her chest. No sign of Ma or Pa, or of Daniel's ma, either, but I heard talk behind the bed curtain. A whimpering come from Miz Ellis's bundle.

I tiptoed close. "Is that my baby?"

She give me a big smile. "Say hello to your baby sister."

A sister! I leaned over. Miz Ellis pulled the blanket off the baby's head. Her skull was shiny and soft. I was afraid to touch her. It looked like I could put my finger right through the skin. The baby pursed up her lips. They went in and out, in and out, like a fish.

"Look, Daniel." I turned around. "I have a sister. Like you."

Daniel's mouth was wide open. What was he staring at? I

followed his eyes. Martha Ellis was holding another bundle, with a foot sticking out the bottom!

I nearly fell down. "Whose baby is that?" I asked.

"Hush," Martha Ellis said. "You boys got no call to be here. Go on back to Daniel's house. You'll upset Mrs. Coombs."

"It's all right, Martha," Miz Ellis whispered. "Let them see."

Martha Ellis brought her bundle to the stump, laid it down, and opened the blanket. I gasped. A naked baby lay inside. It was puny, with little stick arms and legs. It was a boy, I seen that right away, a boy with yellow skin, the color of chicken feet. He stuck his arms out, shivered all over, and then lay still.

"Cover him up!" I said. "Is he dead?"

"He's poorly," Miz Ellis said. "Mrs. Durkee, bring the warm blanket."

The two women wrapped the baby until he was snug. Then they put his other cloth back around him. He never made a sound.

"What's wrong with him?" I asked. I followed Martha Ellis to the fire. She stood near the flames, rocking him.

"He's small and tuckered out. Your ma had a hard travail, birthing two babies," Miz Ellis said. "It's a wonder they survived."

I stared at her. "Ma had two babies at the same time?"

"That's right." Miz Ellis chuckled. "Your ma was brought to bed with twins."

Twins! I couldn't hardly think what that meant. "You mean—I have a sister and a brother?"

Miz Durkee nodded and pursed her lips tight. "Shame on your father for not fetching Kate last night." She dipped some hot water outta the big kettle over the fire and put it in one of Ma's wooden bowls. "Course, the way they talk about Mrs. Tucker up here, it's a wonder she came at all."

I set my hands on my hips. "Pa sent me to git her this morning!"

"Now, now," Miz Ellis said. "Don't fret. I'm sure your ma will thank Mrs. Tucker when she's feeling cleverly again."

Martha Ellis and Miz Durkee give each other funny looks. Did they think Ma might die? My hands felt sweaty all of a sudden.

"Where's Ma?" I asked. "I want to see her."

"Leave her be now," Miz Ellis said. "She's too poorly—"

But she couldn't stop me. Three steps and I was on the other side a the curtain. Miz Tucker and Pa was bent over, tending someone on Ma's pallet. I stared. That weren't my ma. Ma didn't have scratches up and down her arms. Her face weren't that ash color. And she didn't smell bad. Not Ma.

I looked down. Blood everywhere! I gagged. Someone yanked on my coat and pulled me back into the chamber. Martha Ellis hissed like a snake. "Shame on you," she said. "You boys git."

Daniel didn't move. What was wrong with him? He coughed. "I need my mother," he says to the women.

Daniel's ma came out from behind the curtain. He said something in their funny talk, and she gasped and covered her mouth. Then she was jabbering fast.

"Don't speak Indian words in here," I said. "Ma won't like it."

Miz Tucker scowled at me, but she talked English to the other women. "Daniel brought a message from my father," she said. "We'll step outside for a minute. Martha, will you brew up more raspberry-leaf tea? It will help stop the bleeding."

"I will—but we're almost out," Martha Ellis said.

"Can we git more?" I asked.

"Daniel's father can fetch some when he gets back." Miz Tucker started for the door and yanked Daniel after her.

"Wait," I said. "Miz Tucker. Why is my ma bleeding? Will she die?"

No answer.

I followed them into the foreyard. They stood beside Pa's woodpile, jabbering in their funny talk. Miz Tucker looked skairt. Was that on account of Ma? Daniel said that word the old man used, *caw-kont,* that sounded like a crow calling. Had I learned my first word in Pequot? The babies begun wailing and I pulled my hat over my ears. Where could I go? Miz Ellis told me to leave. But no one wanted me at the wigwam, either.

Now they was talking English and Miz Tucker touched something at her waist. She reached under her coat and showed Daniel a pouch. I edged closer. Sure enough, it were like the one I stole, but bigger. Daniel looked ashamed. "I don't have mine," he said. "I lost it."

I got a prickly feeling inside. Miz Tucker's eyes blazed. So she had a temper, too. I wouldn't have thought so, listening to her before.

"Very well," she told Daniel. "I'll use my own pouch to send something to Grandfather—mind you don't lose this one. Wait on me a minute."

Ma screamed and I bit my lip so hard it drew blood. Miz Tucker lifted her skirts and ran for the door, and I slipped in behind her. I pushed past that Ellis woman when she scolded me, dove for my pallet, and rustled under my blankets till I felt the soft deerskin tucked beneath the hemlock boughs. Just a few days since I'd stolen it for Uncle Abner, to prove there was an Injun family next door, but it seemed like months ago. And he'd never even seen it—he'd heard the news about the Tuckers from Ma herself. I shoved the pouch into my britches pocket and hurried for the door.

Miz Tucker caught me as I slipped through the shadows. "Hiram, what are you doing here? I told you to wait outside."

"I forgot something," I said.

"What did you do to your lip? Hold still." She picked up a cloth and wiped blood from my mouth. Then she held my wrist. "Your new brother is very poorly," she said. "So is your ma. Do you want them to get well?"

I thought of the little boy with his stick arms. Thought of

Ma, with her hair all tangled and her mouth twisted. "Yes ma'am," I said.

"Good," she said. "I'll do what I can here, but you must help, too." She gave me her pouch, so much like the one that burned in my pocket. "Give this to Daniel and go to the wigwam. Do what my father tells you. No more foolishness. Understand?"

I nodded. That bad smell filled my nose again and I was glad to get outside. I gulped down the fresh air. Daniel was stamping his feet, like a horse trying to stay warm. When he saw his ma's pouch, he grabbed for it. "Where'd you get this?"

"From your ma," I said. "She says give this to the old man."

Daniel tucked it under his arm and was off running before I could ask what was inside. I hurried after him. Shadows was creeping into the forest and coyotes yipped up on the ridge. "Your old grandfather thinks those crows can talk, don't he?" I asked.

He turned around. His face was shadowy, too. "They warned us of death."

"That's foolish," I said. "They're only birds."

Daniel didn't say nothing, just kept on going. We crossed the tree over the stream, stepping slow and careful with the daylight slipping away.

"Who cooks for you? Who cooks for you-awwll?" called an owl, so close I near fell into the water.

Daniel took off running, like a deer spooked by a hound. "Wait!" I called after him. "What's wrong?"

I run fast as I could to catch him. I thought the sounds would come into my head again, the whooping and hollering, but all I heard was our footsteps, crunching the leaves as we run to the wigwam.

32. Daniel

The call of the owl sent ice trickling under my collar. Was *Cheepi,* the spirit of the dead, hiding in the gloomy shadows? Hiram's heavy footsteps were hard upon mine. In truth, I kept my pace slow, so as not to lose him. I was never so glad to see the open furrows of the wheat field, nor the curls of smoke from house and wigwam.

But wait—what was this? Flames leapt before Grandfather, who stood in the field, arms raised high. He wore his deerskin jacket and leggings. His hair hung loose down his back and the copper pendant glowed on his chest. What was he doing?

When he saw us, his arms drifted down and Rhoda popped up behind him, her eyes lit with the fire.

"Grandfather is singing," she said. "Is the baby all right?"

"There are two babies," I said.

"Two!" Rhoda cried.

"My ma had twins," Hiram said, "a boy and a girl." His chest puffed out like a grouse seeking its mate, but just as fast, his mouth turned down. He stood in front of Grandfather. "The boy is poorly," he said. "Ma is, too. Daniel says the crow talked to you about death. Are they gonna die?"

Hiram's chin trembled. In the days since he'd come to Griswold, I'd only wished him pain. No longer. "Mother needs more physicks," I told Grandfather. "The raspberry leaf is near gone. She wants something else to stop the bleeding—she said you would know."

Grandfather nodded. "What else?"

"Father went to Mr. Durkee's to fetch some firewood, but he'll come here soon to carry new physicks to Hiram's." I pulled the pouch from my pocket and tried to find the right words in Pequot. "If you sing for Mrs. Coombs—" My words were clumsy, so I switched to English. "Mother says, don't tire yourself."

Grandfather took the pouch, loosened the rawhide knot, and felt inside with his forefinger. He drew out a lock of curly red hair.

"That's Ma's!" Hiram grabbed for it, but Grandfather held it above his reach. "You said my ma's name!" Hiram yelled. "I heard you. You're going to cast a spell on her, ain't you? Don't touch her with your witch doctoring."

"Very well." Grandfather set the curls in Hiram's hand and pulled him away from the fire. "Listen to me, Yellow Hair," he said. "I will sing for your mother only if you wish it. My daughter's healing, and the physicks we make, will help her most. Kate has been a doctress for many years. If you had called for her earlier, your mother might not be suffering now."

Hiram snuffled and wiped his nose on his coat. "I know. Ma is too stubborn. She didn't want no Injun—I mean, Indian—doctress in her house." He opened his palm and studied on his mother's hair, as if it could tell him what to do. Rhoda edged close beside me and I took her hand. 'Twas icy cold. We waited.

"Does that singing really work?" Hiram asked at last.

Grandfather set a hand on his shoulder. "Long ago, *powwaws* had great strength," he said. "Our ancestors could swim beneath the ships of the *Owamux* and ruin them. They could take the forms of animals. Or birds. Perhaps those powers remain—perhaps not."

He looked at me, then at Rhoda. We were both trembling. 'Twas not just the cold making us shake. Rhoda's hand was small, cupped tight in my own.

"I am an old man now," Grandfather said. "My skill is fading. But if you wish, Yellow Hair, I will sing for you, and for your family."

"Mother said—" I began, but Grandfather held his hand up to still me.

"Yellow Hair, did you do as I asked?" Grandfather said.

Hiram cut a circle in the muddy furrow with the toe of his boot. He coughed, then wiped his nose. Would he never speak? My toes were near frozen in my moccasins.

"Here," Hiram said. "Take this." He let loose of the lock. It drifted into Grandfather's hand, a red butterfly with curled wings. "I've nothing of value that's mine. But I brought this back." He fished around in his pocket.

I squinted. 'Twas hard to see in the firelight until a rush of sparks lit the quill design. "My pouch!"

I moved to grab it, but Grandfather stilled me with a shake of his head. "Hiram, please explain."

"I stole it." Hiram looked straight at me, bold as can be. "My uncle Abner didn't believe there was an Injun—I mean, that you all was next door. I took this to prove I weren't lying." Blood trickled from his lip. He swiped it away, then looked at each of us in turn. "I ain't a thief—or a liar," he said.

Oh, no? Then what about Mr. Trout? I opened my mouth to speak, but Grandfather shook his head at me.

"It's good you brought this back to Daniel," he said. "Please return it now."

Hiram set the pouch in my hand. Mother's strength poured into my palm through the soft deerskin.

"*Wegun*," I said.

"*Wegun* means 'good'?" Hiram asked. "I learnt me another word?"

Rhoda's teeth clicked and chattered beside me. Grandfather beckoned to her and they disappeared behind the blanket into the wigwam.

"What's he doing?" Hiram asked.

I shrugged. They returned quickly. Grandfather carried his rattle, and Rhoda held Mother's pouch close to her chest.

"Find the raspberry-leaf tea among your mother's physics and add it to the medicine I put in the pouch," Grandfather told Rhoda. "Can you do that? Give it to your father when he comes."

"All right," Rhoda said, but her voice was sad. "I want to stay here."

Grandfather shook his head.

"We'll go to the house," I said. "'Tis bitter cold now."

"What's that rattle for?" Hiram asked.

Grandfather stepped into the firelight. His eyes were far away, as they had been last night. Was he having another fit? "Grandfather," I said. "Mother said—"

Once again, he shook off my words. He set both hands on Rhoda's shoulders, then mine. "Whatever happens, always follow the path," he said to each of us.

"Yes, Grandfather," Rhoda said.

"We will," I told him, but his words made ice in my limbs. *Whatever happens*—did he still fear the crow's message?

Hiram nudged me. "What path? Are we going somewhere else now?"

"Not a real path," I said, but then I held my tongue. That lesson was not for Hiram. I couldn't even puzzle it out myself. I watched Grandfather over my shoulder as we set off in the dark. He shook the rattle, drummed the earth with his feet, and began to sing. His voice was high as the scream of the red-tailed hawk, wild as coyotes calling to one another on the ridge.

"What's he saying?" Hiram asked.

I turned for a last look. The fire lit the pendant on Grandfather's chest. He shook the rattle harder, then beat his chest with his fists. *Swish. Swish. Thrum. Thrum.* His voice rose higher, the drumming came faster, the rattle shivered until I thought it would explode.

Rhoda pulled my sleeve. "He wants to sing by himself."

"I know." I tarried another moment. Mother had said that Grandfather must not tire himself. Should I stop him? But if I did, would it weaken his power? What should I do?

Hiram decided it for me. He plucked at my sleeve. "I've a relish for food," he said. "I've not eaten all day."

My own belly growled an answer, and I heard the sheep below, their sad bleats telling me they were hungry, too. Hiram bolted for the house and Rhoda and I followed close after. Grandfather's mournful cries rang in our ears. I'd never felt so lonesome, even with Rhoda's hand in mine.

33. Hiram

Jody was yipping and barking inside the barn when we pulled the doors open. Them animals drowned out the old man's song. The oxen mooed, the sheep bleated, and the mean gander tucked his head and come after me.

"Git that thing away from me!" I yelled.

"He won't hurt you." Daniel shooed the gander off, but I don't think he favored him much, either.

Daniel set me to work forking hay into the mangers while he milked the cow. *Squirt-splash. Squirt-splash.* The sound kept time with the old man's rattling and drumming. Rhoda plucked eggs from under the hens. The animals made steam, breathing and munching. It was near peaceful in there. We picked seeds from a big sunflower head that hung from the rafters and filled our pockets. I found their privy easily by its smell.

When I come out, Mr. Tucker was there. Rhoda brought funny-looking dried-up roots and leaves from the back chamber and her pa set them in a basket with Miz Tucker's pouch. He hardly said a word, just told us to stir up the fire and stay inside.

Their chamber felt cold and lonesome after he left, and that chanting made me itch, like there was hay chaff down my shirt. Daniel built up the fire and Rhoda lit the tow lamp to chase off the dark. My stomach growled so loud everyone laughed.

"We should eat," Rhoda said, like she was the ma.

She cut up a cold cooked squash and some jonnycake. Daniel went to the back chamber and come back with apples. I dumped the seeds from my pockets and we set into eating. *"Wegun,"* I said. "'Sgood." I cracked a sunflower seed, spit out the husk, and bit down on the kernel.

"I thought you didn't like Indian things," Daniel said.

Was he tricking me? "What do you mean?"

"All this is Indian food," Daniel said. "Corn. Squash. Sunflowers. We had it before the English came."

"What of it?" I pushed the bowl of apples to his side of the table. "Did you have apples?"

Ha! No answer. I'd flummoxed him there.

Rhoda set herself on a stool by the window and pressed up to the glass. I kept my distance. That song was close enough, setting here by the hearth. What was the old man singing, anyway? How could that song help my ma? It sounded like a rabbit snatched up by a coyote. And what about my demons? I hadn't really asked if he could cure me, and I sure didn't feel any different inside. But I'd brought him the pouch. Was that enough?

"I want to sing when I'm older," Rhoda says to Daniel.

"Can girls do a medicine dance?" I asked.

"Perhaps. Grandfather says the old ways are gone, but I could try." She swung around on the stool. "I'd have to be brave and go on a long journey by myself. I couldn't eat for many days. Dreams would send me a message, like the one I had before. I have to wait until I'm older and stronger."

I shook my head. "Why would you want to do all that?"

She held her tongue. She was so small, setting on that stool, yet she talked like a grown person. "Will those physicks work, that your pa carried up the hill?" I asked.

She nodded. "Mother says they will."

"Can't you be a doctress like your ma?" I asked.

"Yes," Rhoda said, "if I want. What about you? What will you do?"

"I don't know," I said. "Tell stories, I guess." I laughed. Why did I say that? The words just popped out.

Daniel scoffed at me, but Rhoda nodded. *"Wegun,"* she said.

"Yes," I said. "My stories will be good ones."

Something screeched louder than the singing. We jumped up. Daniel opened the door and peeked out.

"What's that?" I asked.

"It's the red-tailed hawk," Daniel said.

"Sounds like the one that chased me," I said.

"What do you mean?" Daniel asked.

Should I tell them? They were listening careful, not scowling at me. "When I got loose of the Indians, in the raid, I was running for home," I said. "A hawk come over me, so close I could see its eyes. I ducked down and found a rotten log with a big hole in it. I slid inside—and next thing I knew, those raiders ran right over the top a me. They never saw me."

"That's a good story," Rhoda said.

"It's true!" I said.

"I know." Rhoda smiled. She believed me! "Maybe the hawk saved you."

"I guess. I never thought of it like that."

Rhoda and Daniel give each other a funny look, like they knew a secret. "What's wrong?" I asked.

"A hawk saved us, too," Daniel said. "We followed it into a ravine where Mother discovered a cave. That's where we hid till the raid was over."

"Maybe we saw the same hawk," Rhoda said.

"But we was miles away from each other," I said.

"Hawks fly many miles in a day, looking for prey," Daniel said. He give me a long, serious look. "She must have been the only one to see the whole raid, from beginning to end."

"Not a pretty sight," I said, and held my breath, waiting for the voices—but they didn't come.

Daniel went to the shelf over the fire, took up a piece of wood, and set on the bench, working with his knife. I peered over his shoulder.

"What's that?" I asked.

"A doll for Rhoda," he said.

It didn't look like much yet, but I could see a round part for the head and some square feet. "Is it a boy?" I asked.

"A girl," Rhoda said. "She needs a name."

Names. I thought on my new brother, so cold and gray on the plank table. Of my sister in her blanket. If the babies lived, they'd need names. And dolls, too. A boy and a girl. Would Daniel make them for me?

I durst not ask. Not yet.

34. Daniel

Jody's bark sent me to my feet before I was even awake. I hardly knew where I was. Rhoda's doll, near finished but for smoothing, lay on the plank table beside my knife. An ugly great pain had settled in my back, from sleeping on the bench.

"Who is it, girl?"

Jody's tail wagged and Father came in, bearing a small torch. His beard pointed in strange directions and his hair was rumpled as he pulled off his hat. He set the torch on the hearth and raked up the coals. "Where's Rhoda?" he whispered.

"In your bed. Hiram's in the loft." I rubbed my shoulders to ease their cramping. "Is Mrs. Coombs all right?"

"Your mother says she's doing cleverly, though she's very fatigued. Kate's physics did the trick."

And the singing, perhaps, but of course Father didn't know about Grandfather.

"The little boy is poorly," Father said. "Mother will stay the night with him. Is your grandfather all right?"

"I don't know. He was up to the wigwam."

"I came home along the road; 'twas easier to find my way in the dark. Perhaps we should look in on him, since he wasn't well last night." Father sighed and reached for his hat. "I'm all tuckered out."

"I'll go."

"Thank you, Daniel," Father said. "You're a comfort to me." He sank onto the bench.

A comfort to Father? He surprised me. I snapped my fingers, called Jody over, and went outside, carrying the torch. A new moon was setting, cutting a thumbnail slice in the black sky. The night was silent. No song from the hilltop. No wind. Only my footsteps, and Jody's snuffling on the wet ground.

The wigwam stood open to the night. Had Grandfather

forgotten to drop his blanket? I sniffed. No scent of smoke. I lifted the torch and peered inside. The wigwam was empty.

"Grandfather?"

Silence.

Jody growled near the edge of the woods and ran to me, whimpering. "What's this? Show me, girl." She nipped my pants, then dashed away. I followed her to the edge of the timber, lifting the torch high—and saw a dark, tumbled shape.

"Grandfather!" He lay flat on the wheat stubble. Deerskin jacket open to the night. Hair swirling around him like tangled grass. Eyes half open, staring at the dark.

I knelt beside him. As in his fit the other night, his face was twisted as though he'd seen some horror. Had *Cheepi* passed here? My teeth chattered and my hands shook so I nearly dropped the torch.

I set the torch into the soft ground. What would Mother do? I slid my hand inside the jacket to feel his chest. "Please," I whispered. A flutter beneath my fingers: he lived! I chafed his wrists as Mother did when someone was feverish. His hands were ice. Grandfather moaned.

"'Tis me, Daniel," I told him. "Wake up! Please." I slipped my hands beneath his armpits but couldn't move him. What should I do?

Jody licked Grandfather's face, then mine. "Jody—go home!" I jumped to my feet, pushed her toward the house. "Get Father. Go!"

She whimpered, tucked her tail between her legs, scurried away. I hoisted the torch and went into the wigwam, working fast. Set the torch on the stone hearth, tore the blanket from the door, gathered the wolf skin, hurried back to Grandfather. Jody's bark echoed from the house. "Good dog," I whispered. I cupped my hands around my mouth and hailed Father. He whistled back.

"Father is coming," I told Grandfather. Could the old man hear me, or make any sense of my words?

I lifted his shoulders and wedged the wolf skin beneath his back, then his hips and legs, to keep his body from the cold ground. I spoke to him as I worked. "Your black wolf will warm you. And your blanket. I'll tuck it over your feet."

I saw his face through a blur of tears. I thought on the owl hooting; remembered how *Kaukont* cawed and left his feather behind. "Don't die, Grandfather," I said. "We haven't finished my lessons. We must carve the dugout. Rhoda wants to learn your singing. Don't let *Cheepi* come near."

No answer. Footsteps thumped up the hill. I hoisted the torch and called out. "Father! Over here!"

Father ran with heavy steps, Rhoda clinging to his back and Hiram following behind. "They're coming," I told Grandfather. "We'll carry you inside."

Grandfather groaned and opened his eyes. I dropped to my knees. His mouth moved and a strange gurgling sound came out. I cocked my head so my ear touched his lips. "Tell me again," I said.

"Don't . . . move me," Grandfather moaned. He murmured in Pequot this time. "Stay here. Not wigwam."

I took his face in my hands. "But it's cold. Mother will bring you her physicks."

Grandfather's eyes bulged like a frog's. "Don't *move* me!"

Father and Hiram breathed heavily behind me, but I stayed close to Grandfather. "You'll be all right," I told him, though I didn't believe it.

"Bury me . . . here," Grandfather said. Each word came like a nail pried from a plank: wrenching and slow. "Southwest. Toward *Cautantowwit*. With the wolf skin . . ."

"No," I said. "You won't die. We'll care for you."

His hand clawed at me. "Don't move . . . the stones . . . after. Danger . . . will come."

"The stones? What stones?"

"Hush." Father dropped to one knee beside me. "Grandfather, you must not speak. You've had another fit. Save your strength."

Rhoda crouched at Grandfather's waist. She took his rough hands in her small ones and rubbed them. "Can you lift your arms, Grandfather?" she asked.

He grunted. One hand moved while the other stayed still on the blanket.

"Is he going to die?" Hiram asked. He stood hidden in the shadows.

"I hope not," Father said. "Think we can move him into the wigwam?"

"He wants to stay here," I said.

Grandfather's eyes fluttered closed. "Kate," he said. A great shiver shook him from head to foot.

Father gripped Grandfather's wrist. "His heart still beats. I'll fetch Kate. Daniel, stay here with Rhoda and Jody. Perhaps 'tis best not to move him, as he asks. You have wrapped him up warm. Hiram, come with me. Your pa wants you home." Father passed the back of his hand over his eyes. "Poor Kate. I don't know where she'll find the strength . . ." His words drifted away as he took up the torch.

Hiram bent to touch Grandfather's foot beneath the blanket. "You ain't no witch. Thanks for singing." He disappeared after Father, leaving Rhoda and me alone in the dark. We sat on each side of Grandfather, holding his hands to keep him warm. Rhoda chanted the songs she had learned from Grandfather these last few days. Jody curled up at his feet. It seemed a great while before the moon sank behind the mountains and hoofbeats sounded, bringing voices and a bark from Jody.

"Mother's here," I told Grandfather.

Mother slid off the mare and fell to her knees. "Father!" she cried.

Grandfather started and gazed up at her, as if he heard the scream with his eyes. His mouth opened on one side, pouring strange words into the night. Mother set her ear to his mouth, then shook her head. "He makes no sense," she said.

The mare snorted and whinnied. "Rabbit knows that Grandfather is hurt," Rhoda said. Father nodded and led the mare away, tying her to the lone oak.

"Shall we move him to the house?" Father asked.

Mother shook her head. She gazed up at me. "Did he sing?" she asked.

I nodded. "He danced, and drummed with his feet, and shook the rattle." Tears thickened my voice. "I tried to tell him what you said, to take care and not tire himself—but he wouldn't listen."

She held Grandfather's hands tight and spoke to him in Pequot. "Father," she said. "Come back. The mother will live, and the twins, too. Our physicks have helped them to mend. Come back now."

"Where did Grandfather go?" Rhoda asked.

"A great distance," Mother said. "They go far away when they sing."

I shivered. "An owl hooted at us in the forest."

"Yes," Mother said. "And we heard the red-tailed hawk, crying out in the dark. 'Twas strange."

She stroked Grandfather's cheeks, then his forehead. Grandfather never opened his eyes.

We sat with him through the night. Mother fetched salves from the house to rub on his chest, brewed hot toddies and foul-smelling physicks, but Grandfather could neither sip nor swallow. Father built a fire atop the wheat stubble and wrapped us in blankets as the cold settled deep in our bones. Rhoda and I leaned up against Father. Sleep nipped my eyes, but I chased it away.

When gray light crept over the hilltop, Grandfather lay still. I thought on the lesson he had given us. Grandfather Turtle would soon carry the sun from the east again. Perhaps Grandfather would not die? Then Mother's fingers scurried like a mouse onto Grandfather's wrist. She gasped. Tore open his jacket and set her ear on his chest. Held her palm before his mouth. Sat up on her knees and howled the cry of a lonesome wolf. Rhoda screamed and burrowed into Father's jacket. He covered his face with his hands. I hugged myself and rocked back and forth, my eyes on Grandfather.

I had seen death in the forest, when Father and I shot turkeys. Had felt the stilled heart of Mr. Trout when I scooped him from the stream and finished his life with a stone. Had watched Father kill biddies and Mother skin a deer.

But this was Grandfather. Who had been with us only a few weeks. Who had given us his lessons—

My breath quickened. I reached for Grandfather's hand, felt its cold emptiness. His last lesson was about death. What had he told us about the spirit world?

I strained to remember. Perhaps when *Kaukont* brought the warning, he foretold the death of Grandfather himself.

And he knew. I was sure of it. Grandfather knew he would never dance or sing again.

35. Daniel

We waited with Grandfather while Father went to fetch the sledge. "Why did he want to die outside?" I asked. "The wigwam was his home."

"If a man dies inside the wigwam, we must burn it after," Mother said. Her hand smoothed my hair, over and over. "I think he meant for you to have it."

"I don't want the wigwam," Rhoda cried. "I only want Grandfather."

"He spoke about *Cautantowwit*," I said.

"Yes, we lie facing the southwest," Mother said, "where our corn and beans come from." She cupped her hand under my chin, turned my face to her own. "Did he speak of death any other time?"

"When he gave us lessons, in the wigwam, he spoke of the spirit world," I said.

She was still. "'Tis as I thought, then," she said.

"What do you mean?"

"He was already ill when he left his home. This was why he came—to see you and Rhoda before he was gone."

"But he tired himself singing. 'Tis my fault. He wouldn't listen to me."

"You're not to blame," Mother said. "Think of his fit the other night. His hands trembled even when he arrived— and sometimes, his vision seemed to fail him."

She was right; I had seen that.

"Perhaps he sang for his own death," Mother said. "The herbs he sent for Mrs. Coombs stopped her bleeding. His physicks helped to save her."

"You helped, too," Rhoda said.

"So did you," Mother said. "She drank all of your raspberry-leaf tea."

First light warmed my back. I heard the plodding steps of the oxen, the creak of the sledge as Father approached. Mother rose, but I held on to her skirt. "Grandfather said one other thing." I closed my eyes, waiting to hear the words, which came to me as if Grandfather himself stood behind me. "He said we must not move . . . the stones. And then he said: 'Danger will come.' What stones? What did he mean?"

"When someone dies, we place stones over his grave." Mother drew her shawl tight across her chest. "We must never move them. It is wrong to disturb the dead. That is his last lesson." She lifted Rhoda to her feet. "Go to the house now, and rest. Father and I will bring him home."

We stumbled down the hill. Jack Frost had bitten very hard in the night, coating the grass in silver, just as he had on the day Grandfather came to us. We passed through the front chamber. Climbed into Mother and Father's bed. Pulled up the quilt. Huddled close for comfort and warmth.

Rhoda slept hard, but I paddled between sleep and waking. Strange sounds filled the front chamber. Doors slamming; wood scraping on wood; Jody whimpering. And worst of all, Mother's soft weeping, seeping into the chinking in the walls.

Then came a sudden cry from Father, and Jody's sharp bark. Something clattered to the floor. What now? The corn husks rustled as I jumped from the bed, and Rhoda woke. I peered around the curtain and stared.

A strange woman stood at the table, hands spread wide

on the planks to hold herself up. Soot covered her face. Father stared at the floor and my eyes followed his gaze. Swathes of hair, like black wheat cut with the scythe, littered the puncheon floor. Skeins of hair, longer than a horse's tail, longer than Rhoda's braids.

I felt buffle brained. 'Twas like Mother's hair.

"Mother!" Rhoda screamed and dove under the quilt.

I tried to hold her, but she only burrowed deeper. "'Tis all right. Rhoda, don't be afraid." But I was frightened, too.

The curtain opened and I scrambled away. Was this Mother, or some vision of *Cheepi?* She smelled of smoke, and of that terrible stench from Hiram's front chamber.

"Rhoda. Daniel. Be still. Let me speak."

"Go away!" Rhoda's voice was muffled under the quilt. Mother searched under the covers for Rhoda's hands.

"Come here!" Mother cried.

My arms went around my sister. "Don't shout!" I said. "You're giving her a fright."

"Kate." Father came to the foot of the bed. Mother's glossy hair streamed from his fingers. "Kate, how could you do this? Destroy your beauty? Look on yourself!"

Tears washed tracks through the soot on Mother's face. "You know it is our way," she said, "the way we show our grief."

"How did you cut it?" Father asked.

In an instant, I knew the answer. I touched my leather sheath, found it empty, scrambled from the bed and into the chamber. The knife lay gleaming on the plank boards. I wiped it on my breeches, put it where it belonged, then came back to the bed. "Don't touch Rhoda's braids," I said. My hand went to my own hair, tangled below my collar. "Or mine."

"Rhoda is too young to cut her hair," Mother said. "You may do as you please." She held my face with her sooty hands. Though I tried to twist away, she would not free me. "You must choose your own way to honor Grandfather." She released me and gathered her hair from Father's open hands. "My hair will grow again," she said, "but my father will not come back. I have only my sorrow."

She stumbled toward the back chamber. Grandfather must be in there now. Though I'd sat with him under the stars all night, I was afraid to stay in the house with his body when his spirit had flown away.

Father must have read my thoughts. "I need help to build a proper box for your grandfather," he said. "We have no wood, and there is nary a shilling in Mother's coin basket."

I stood tall. I knew what to do. "I will find the wood," I said.

Rhoda wiped her face with the hem of her skirt. "I'll come with you," she said.

36. Hiram

"The old man sang for us," I told Pa when I come home. "He sent physics for Ma. Now he's laying sick on the ground."

Pa didn't pay me no mind. He sat in our only chair, shaking his head and pulling on his ear like he couldn't believe the sounds in the chamber.

"Two babies," he said. "Who would a thought. Twins. And they say your ma is safe now."

"When can I see her?"

Pa didn't answer. He begun to snore, sitting straight up. Where was I going to sleep? The chamber was still crowded with women and babies. Miz Ellis was asleep on the stump, with her skirts spread out like a tablecloth. I put some wood on the fire, pulled my pallet into a corner, and flopped down. I was cold, so far from the hearth, but I didn't notice. I fell asleep fast.

Next time I moved, a patch of sun crossed my face and Pa was shaking my shoulder. Someone howled, but it weren't Ma or Pa.

"What's wrong?" I sat right up.

"Easy," Pa whispered. "Your brother is squalling because he's hungry, that's all. Fetch some wood, will you?"

I stumbled out. Frost winked on the ground. My breath made smoke as I carried wood and piled it on the hearth. I had to dodge them women every time I crossed the chamber. One was walking a baby around, another one was heating water, another was tending Ma behind the curtains. I tried to peek at my new brother and sister, but the women wouldn't let me near.

"When can I see Ma?" I asked Pa.

"Not now," Pa said. "She needs to rest. Why don't you go

on down to Daniel's? His pa said you'd be welcome there today."

"But the old man—"

Ma called out to Pa behind her curtain and he was gone before I could say a word. Miz Ellis give me an apple and a piece of jonnycake and shooed me away. "Go see your friend," she said. "When you come home, your ma will be doing cleverly."

Was Daniel my friend? I weren't sure, but I went off anyway.

I was on the far side a the brook and almost to the pasture when I thought of the grandfather. What if he was still laying on the ground? I crept up slow and careful and peeked over the wall. Nothing. No one on the frosty grass. I climbed over the wall and listened. No sound from the wigwam. I didn't dare look in. I circled around it and run down the hill.

The dog gave a lonesome howl inside the house. Smoke come out the chimbley. I started for the door when I seen Daniel and Rhoda walking down the trail to the road. They was holding hands.

I hailed them. "Where you going?"

They turned around. That same minute, the door opened, and a ghost stood there. A ghost with a gray face, chopped-off hair, big, staring eyes. Just like in one of them bad dreams, my feet was fixed to the frozen ruts in the trail. And then I was running and screaming with my arms flailing and my feet stumbling. I clapped my hands over my ears, sure the sounds would come after me, but I heard naught but my own voice yelling, "Daniel! Rhoda! There's a ghost!"

They stood waiting. Had that ghost put a spell on them?

"Go on, git!" I couldn't hardly get the words out when I caught up. I pushed them toward the road. "Run! There's a ghost in your house."

Their eyes was red, their mouths pulled down. They didn't budge.

"That's Mother," Rhoda said, her voice so small, I couldn't hardly hear her. "She cut off her hair."

"Why?" I asked. "What's she got on her face?"

"Ashes," Daniel said. "Grandfather died."

"He's dead?" I looked back at the house. The door was closed. "Where is he?" I asked.

"In the back chamber," Daniel told me. "We're going to get wood for the coffin." He looked at his moccasins, and then he surprised me. "Come along," he said.

"All right." I wanted to ask why Miz Tucker did that to herself, and where would they bury the old man, and who was going to build the coffin, but I could see they didn't want no questions. Rhoda kept hold of Daniel's hand and I followed behind. Would my own sister walk with me like that when she was bigger?

Like she heard me thinking, Rhoda looked over her shoulder. "What did you name your babies?" she asked.

I stopped right there. "I don't know," I told her. "I guess Ma and Pa didn't decide yet."

We kept going down a steep hill and across the river. *My babies.* She give me an idea. It grew in my chest and made me walk tall. I thought of the twins, especially the girl, with her soft scalp that breathed in and out. Ma might say no. But not Pa. I ducked my chin so Daniel and Rhoda wouldn't catch me grinning.

37. Daniel

We stood in the cooper's foreyard. A pile of new barrels was stacked up beside his workshop. What if Mr. Sykes didn't remember me? I rapped on the door.

Mr. Sykes greeted us with a wide smile. "Why, young Daniel! What are you doing about so early? And you've brought some friends."

I couldn't speak. Rhoda stepped up beside me. "I'm Rhoda. This is Hiram, our neighbor. Our grandfather died," she said.

"What a shame. Come inside, please." Mr. Sykes drew us in, closed the door, sat us by the fire on overturned barrels. "What happened?"

My voice was still caught in my throat. Rhoda told the story quickly. "Grandfather had some fits. And he went far away when he sang. He can't come back," she said.

"But he saved Ma and my new babies with his medicines," Hiram said.

I stared at him. Did he really say that? When we first met at the fish weir, Hiram's mouth had been twisted in a sneer, and his words about all of us were poison. He seemed a different boy now.

I hoped to learn.

When the coffin was finished, Mr. Sykes set a hand on my shoulder. "Your parents can fetch the box when they're ready."

We thanked him and set off for home. My legs felt like ash splints: thin and wobbly. Rhoda whined as we climbed the steep hill. Hiram pointed to his back. "Climb up, Rhoda. I can carry you."

Rhoda scrambled onto his back and wrapped her arms around his neck. I was too worn out to feel jealous. Besides, Hiram didn't last long. Halfway home, he let Rhoda slip down. "You're too heavy," he said.

"No I'm not," Rhoda said. "Here. Let me hold your hands."

She took my hand, then Hiram's, and walked between us. Together, we hoisted her over the steep parts. We stayed quiet. I was glad for Rhoda's hand, tight in my own. I looked across her dark head at Hiram. My sister had hitched us together, like a railing tied to two fence posts.

Grandfather would be glad. Hot tears filled my eyes and made me stumble as I followed the trail up the hill.

38. Hiram

Seemed like all the noise and bustle had moved from my house to Daniel's. The door kept opening and closing. The

Ellis men stomped in and told Mr. Tucker they'd go fetch the coffin. Miz Ellis followed them in. She shrieked when she seen Miz Tucker.

"Kate!" she yelled. "What have you done!" She flopped down on the bench and covered her face with her apron. "Twins at the Coombses'. Your father dead by daybreak! It's too much for my old brain to take in."

Too much for my brain, too. People I'd never seen was coming in with food and cider. They all give Daniel's ma funny looks when they seen her face, but most didn't say much about it.

Daniel and I snatched some jonnycake from the table when no one was looking. "Who are these folks?" I asked him.

"Neighbors," he said. "People Mother has doctored."

I felt ashamed all over again, thinking how I'd once insulted his ma.

When Miz Tucker said she needed help washing the old man's body, and Mr. Tucker sent Daniel for shovels to dig the grave, my thoughts turned to the raid and our dead neighbor with his staring eyes. I set off for home before the noises could come after me, but it was quiet inside my head.

I stood in the meadow ground alone, listening. The raid was gone. I heard nothing but the gander, hissing and honking. And the wind in the timber.

All was quiet to home, too. Finally. Martha Ellis, she that was so cross yesterday, even spoke kindly this time. She was the only one left tending to things. "The babies are doing cleverly," she said.

I pulled back the curtain. There was Ma, all cleaned up, her red hair spread out on the pallet and her face whiter than the frost on the ground—but she give me a small smile just the same. Them babies was on each side of her, sound asleep.

"Hello, Ma," I said.

"Hiram," she said. "We have twins."

"I know." I studied them. They was shriveled up and red. The boy was the smaller one. I touched his little fist. "What's his name?" I asked.

"Reuben," she said. "We haven't named your sister yet."

My sister. My brother. I liked that. I run one finger over my sister's cheek and her lips kissed the air. I laughed. "Where's Pa?" I asked.

"Fetching water," Ma said. "Leave me be now. I'm done in." Her eyes fluttered like a butterfly's wings. I thought she was asleep, but then she fixed her eyes on me again. "Who was that woman helped me last night? She saved my life."

"Don't you know?" I asked. "That was Daniel's ma. Miz Tucker."

Ma's eyes opened wide and I laughed out loud. Before she could say anything, I ran to find Pa.

He was coming up the path with the water buckets. I told him everything. How the old man sang for Ma and fixed some medicines. How we'd built the coffin with Mr. Sykes. How Daniel and his pa were fixing to dig the grave.

Pa set the buckets down. "Digging the grave alone?"

I pulled up my collar. "I reckon."

For once, he believed me. "Fetch our shovels," Pa said.

I showed Pa the path through the woods to Daniel's house. As we walked, I told him my idea. He didn't say yes, but he didn't say no, either. "We'll see what your ma thinks," he said.

"Too bad Uncle Abner don't know how Miz Tucker saved Ma's life," I said.

Pa stopped walking and rubbed his chin. "It wouldn't make a bit of difference. Your uncle's got blinders on his eyes, just like an old workhorse."

I tried to picture my uncle with blinders on either side of his head. It made me sad, same as it does when I seen a horse that way. I was glad Uncle Abner was gone—and maybe Ma was, too. She hadn't said his name in a while.

Shovels thumped as we come near the wall. There was already a hole in the ground up to Mr. Tucker's knees. He was tossing the dirt out with Mr. Sykes. Mr. Durkee and the blacksmith was waiting their turn. Daniel and the Ellis men piled up dirt at one end of the hole.

"Why did so many people come?" I asked Pa.

"Bad tidings travel faster than good ones," Pa said, and climbed over the wall. He raised his hat high. "Good day," Pa called. "Thought you might need some help."

The men all stopped and stared at him. I held my breath. Some of those men drove Uncle Abner away. Would they be mad at Pa and me? But Mr. Tucker lifted his hat and said, "Thank you. We appreciate it."

Mr. Sykes waved to me. "Hiram," he called. "Another hard worker. Come along."

Pa's eyebrows raised up when Mr. Sykes said that. I smiled and went over to help Daniel pile the dirt.

There weren't much talk, just digging. The hole got deeper as the men took turns climbing inside. I was glad they didn't send me down in there.

Daniel stopped shoveling and stared off at the mountains. I looked but didn't see nothing interesting—just the hills and the gray sky. A chipmunk chattered. The wind sighed in the trees.

"Grandfather will like it here," Daniel said.

I stared at that hole in the ground. I thought of the old man laying in the box we made. Would he be scared under the dirt? "Seems lonesome to me," I said.

I waited for Daniel to be mad at me, to tell me I'm buffle brained, the way he usually did. Instead, he said, "Yes. It is lonesome." His mouth turned down.

I picked up a stick and broke it into little pieces. I tossed them into the field one at a time. "We could play in the wigwam sometimes," I said. "We'll bring Rhoda, and my babies, when they're older. I'll tell a story. If he hears us talking, he won't be lonely."

Daniel sent me a long slow look that made me think of the old man. "Maybe," he said.

I think he meant yes.

39. Daniel

We buried Grandfather near candle-lighting time, with the neighbors gathered around. He was wrapped in his wolf skin, as he had asked. Mother set his favorite things around him before we closed the box. His deerskin shoulder bag. The fox quiver. Corn kernels for food on the journey.

I set the war club by his side. "For protection," I said. I'd no use for it now.

Mother sang Pequot prayers over the coffin, holding Rhoda close, and then Father read from our psalter. Each person took a turn with the shovel, scattering dirt onto the box. I waited while Mr. Chase said a prayer, and while Father took the shovel and spoke with a broken voice. "Thank you, Grandfather, for your teachings," he said. "I'm sorry you were gone so fast."

The shovel came to me and I struggled to find my words. I turned my back to the neighbors, opened my jacket, and leaned over the grave, to show Grandfather the wampum belt cinched tight around my waist. I spoke in Pequot, though my words faltered. "It was good you came to us, Grandfather. I'll miss you. How can I build the canoe now? I will try to follow the right path—if you help me."

I waited. Would Grandfather answer? The hilltop was silent, save for the heavy breathing of the neighbors. 'Twas too hard to shovel dirt on Grandfather's box. I passed the shovel to Mr. Chase, but Hiram grabbed it first.

"Wait," he said. He scooped up a pile of dirt, then staggered to the hole. "This is Yellow Hair, saying good-bye to Gray Hair."

I tucked my chin to hide my smile. Grandfather would give his deep raspy laugh if he knew Hiram called him this name.

But what was this? Hiram had more to say. "I'm glad you learnt me to build a wigwam. And thank you for taking the noises away." Dirt tumbled into the hole.

Grandfather had said that demons lived inside Hiram. Had he chased them away, when he sang, or had Hiram fought off the demons himself? It didn't matter. My cheeks grew warm. I had called Hiram a gander head and a buffle brain. He had spat on me, called me a dirty Injun. All those names tumbled into the hole where Grandfather lay.

Show me, Grandfather. Show me the way to the path. Teach me who I am.

But how could he? Each man lifted his shovel. Dirt rained down on the coffin, covering the soft, smooth pine. Grandfather would never hear me, under the ground. Or would he? Hiram thought he might.

Thump. Thump. Every shovel load made me flinch.

When the soil was mounded over the coffin, Mr. Sykes and the blacksmith hoisted three heavy stones from the wall and set them over the grave. The biggest was a lumpy white quartz, streaked with pink. Grandfather would like that one. I found Mother's eyes and she nodded. So these were the stones that should never be moved. Their weight settled in my chest.

Rhoda moved away from Mother, slid her fingers from her mouth, and began to sing the tune Grandfather had chanted in the wigwam only yesterday. Everyone stared at her, but she paid them no mind. She opened her coat. Grandfather's copper pendant gleamed on her dress.

'Twas fitting that she should have it. I touched the wampum belt.

Rhoda's voice rose and a shadow flitted over us.

"Kee-er! Kee-er!" The red-tailed hawk rose from a low branch on the oak tree, its talons outstretched. Had it been watching all this time? The red fan of its tail feathers spread as it tipped its wings.

"Grandfather!" Rhoda screamed. Her knees buckled as the hawk swooped over us. The men ducked and clapped on their hats, to keep its talons from their hair. Hiram gawked at the bird as if he'd seen a ghost. Father scooped Rhoda into his arms and held her against him. The hawk flew out over the wheat field and sailed down the valley, drifting on currents of wind toward the river and on to the ridgeline in the west.

Thank you, Grandfather.

Someone coughed; another man spoke softly. The neighbors drifted away, but I stayed fixed as the men tipped hats to Mother, spoke to Father, took hold of their wives. The women pulled shawls and bonnets tight. A hand settled on my shoulder and I looked up at Mr. Sykes.

"I'm sorry I never met your grandfather." He pointed to the hawk, winging into the dusk. "Or perhaps I did."

I found a smile for him. "Grandfather was good at building things," I said.

"Like his grandson." Mr. Sykes smiled. "Tomorrow you should be with your family. I keep the Sabbath the next day—so I'll expect you on Monday, if your parents can spare you."

"Yes," I told him. "I'll be there."

I touched my hat and watched as he strode away. I had said naught to Father or Mother about my plan. Father couldn't say no, could he? We had to pay for the wood. And I'd not work there forever—

Or would I?

I thought on the cooper's shop, each tool in its own place, the sweet smell of new wood mingling with smoke. I'd never be a teacher, like Father. Nor a doctress, like Mother and Rhoda. Nor a *powwaw*. Grandfather knew that.

But I *could* learn to make things. Barrels, perhaps. A canoe. More dolls for my sister.

I turned my face to the sky. The first star winked in the growing dark.

A jab in my ribs made me jump.

"Hey, you asleep?" Hiram poked me again. "How long will your ma look so strange? Why'd she cut her hair like that, anyway?"

I almost spoke to him sharp, but something stopped me. His eyes weren't buffle brained. Just curious. He wanted to know. That was all.

"When someone dies, Pequot people cut their hair and smear ashes on their faces. 'Tis a way to show we are sad."

"Then why don't you cut *your* hair?" Hiram asked.

I thought on it while the neighbors drifted down the hill, while Father and Mother grew shadowy in the dusk. "Mother said 'twas up to me, what I do," I told him. But that was not all. I looked at him, straight on. "I'm part Pequot," I said. "And part English, like you."

Hiram spat on the ground. "We ain't dirty Tories!" he said. "We're Scotch-Irish. So there."

I come near to laughing but caught myself. I shouldn't smile, with Grandfather so cold in the ground. Should I?

"Hiram! Come along now," Mr. Coombs called.

Hiram raised his hand. "See you tomorrow," he said. "You can learn me more of those funny words your grandfather knew. And I'll tell you a story."

"All right." Was I ready to be Hiram's friend?

His yellow head shone as he turned away. Then he spun on his heel and called to me. "Those babies are crying like all get-out," he said. "Your ma sure made them noisy."

Hiram picked a funny way to say thank-you. I waved to him just the same.

40. Daniel

I slipped belly bump down the ladder next morning, well past first light.

Mother sat near the hearth, weaving another basket. A pile of splints lay at her feet, some pale white, others a dark honey color. Soot still covered Mother's face. Her eyes were set in deep hollows and her hair was jagged on her collar.

If only I were as small as Rhoda and could slide into her lap, set my head on her shoulder! Would she stroke my hair, wipe my tears? I started toward her, then stopped. Mother seemed like the doll I'd made for Rhoda, barely alive.

I glanced at the bench, half looking for Grandfather, though I knew 'twas foolish to expect him. He should be here, cutting corn from the cob, grumbling that Mother had pushed him into a woman's job. The room was lonesome without him.

Mother looked up from her work. She seemed startled, as if she hadn't seen me come in. She nodded toward the plank table. "I found something for you in Grandfather's things."

I hefted a strange, heavy tool with a sharp blade and a curved handle shaped to fit my palm. "What is it?"

"A tool for making a canoe. You use it to smooth and plane the wood of the dugout, once you have burned out the inside of the log. I believe he was saving it till you made the canoe together."

"'Tis unfair!" I slammed the tool down, shaking the table. "I can never make the canoe now. Not without Grandfather. He died too soon! We never picked our tree!"

"I know." Mother lifted another splint, gave it an odd look, and set it on her lap, as if she'd forgotten what to do with it. She reached for my hand and pulled me close while I wept.

I wiped my face on my sleeve. "Do you know how to build a canoe?" I asked.

She cocked her head like a small bird. "'Tis so long since I watched my brothers make one, but I believe I can still remember. Perhaps Mr. Sykes would help us?"

Us. That word lifted my spirits. "Abenakis make birch bark canoes."

"True. But he may know something of dugouts as well," Mother said.

"What kind of tree would you use?" Father stood in the shed doorway, carrying a brimming bucket of milk. I hadn't heard him come in.

"Grandfather said chestnut is best," I told him.

"A fine idea." Father set his bucket down and pulled off gloves and hat. "Chestnut won't rot. A tall straight one grows near the gate."

"Would you help me to hollow it out?" I asked. "Grandfather told me how to burn the inside."

Father came to me. Set one hand on my shoulder. "Only if you promise me one thing."

I waited, leaning against him.

"Promise, when you launch it, you won't go far from us. We need you here."

"I promise." I was too shy to meet his gaze, but his words warmed me. "I only want to fish in the river, for trout and shad."

Mother's hands began to move and I watched her a moment. Her fingers snaked a pale splint into the half-formed basket, twining the ash in and out through darker splints so the pattern alternated, dark, then light. Dark. Light. Mother. Father. A dark splint, a light one, woven together. My sister and me, formed from the two—each one of us a sturdy basket, held by the tight mesh of our parents' weaving. Each neither Pequot, nor English, but both.

As if she'd heard my thoughts, Rhoda's footsteps sounded in the loft, then came pit-pat into the chamber. Her hair was in tangles, her eyes caked with sleep and tears. "Where is Daniel going?" she asked. Her voice quivered.

"I'm staying right here," I said.

"Sit with me." Mother set her splints aside and pulled Rhoda onto her lap. She reached for her wooden comb and drew it gently through Rhoda's tangles.

A knock sounded at the door. Father smiled. "There's a visitor thinks you're going *some*where this morning," he said.

I sighed, though in truth, I was pleased. I opened the

door and gazed out over Hiram's yellow head. The sky was a deep blue above the mountains. A good day to start on the dugout.

"Today I'm choosing the tree for my canoe," I told Hiram.

Hiram rubbed his eyes. "What canoe?"

"The one I'm—" I near said *the one I'm building with Grandfather.* I took a breath, started again. "The dugout we will make this winter. A Pequot canoe."

Hiram dug his toe into the dirt by the front step. "How can you build it without your grandfather?"

"'Twill be hard," I said, "but Mother will help me. She knows what to do." I took a deep breath. "Building takes figuring. You can help me with that part."

"Where's the tree? I can help to build it, too."

I smiled, remembering. "Grandfather said you might be bored."

"I won't." Hiram scowled. "I worked to make the wigwam, didn't I?" His frown slid into a grin. "'Sides, nothin's more boring than babies. Every time I set down, Pa sends me to the woods to find walnuts for that smelly milk he makes for Lila Kate." He wrinkled up his nose.

"Who's Lila Kate?" Rhoda called out from Mother's lap.

"My new sister." Hiram squared his shoulders. "Was my idea to name her Kate, on account of Miz Tucker saving the twins. Ma said that was just right. The boy is called Reuben."

Mrs. Coombs named her daughter *Kate?* Mother's hands stilled, combing Rhoda's hair, and her face lit for the first time since Grandfather died. "Well. Isn't that fine," she said.

"Close the door, boys," Father said. "You're letting all of November into the chamber."

I beckoned to Rhoda. She looked small and sad, perched on Mother's knee. "Come on," I told her. "Find your warm clothes. You can help us, too."

Rhoda gave me a broken smile. She slid from Mother's lap and ran for her boots and shawl.

I breathed deep and stepped out into the bright, sharp morning.

Witness

Years pass.
Roads hug the river.
Smoke from many fires
twists into the welcoming bowl
of the sky.

A hawk carves slow loops
above flocks of sheep
nibbling on clipped pastures;
she sails above hay fields
stretched tight as bedsheets
from ridgeline to valley floor.
Riding the updraft,
the hawk carries these mountains
deep within her swift, light bones.

Her circles narrow.
One man emerges from the timber,
lifts his hat above a thinning thatch
of yellow hair.
Another crosses the wheat stubble
in worn moccasins;
raises a dark hand in greeting.

The flash of a scythe
pulls the hawk to the oak.

Talons outstretched,
she settles on a weighted branch.
Hooded eyes watch
for vole, weasel, deer mouse,
to dart before the swinging blade.

Sturdy hardhack, ragweed,
oat straw and brambles
fall to the scythe.
The tall man sinks to one knee.
Purple beads glint at his waist
as he pulls tangled grass
from a hidden boulder.
Snip snip.
His clippers reveal white quartz,
streaked with pink,
a craggy headstone
cradled by the ground.

The hawk feels the shift
when the oak leaves—
burnished and brittle—
rattle in a sudden wind.
Thunder rumbles on the far side of the valley.
The hawk lifts in silence
as a single bruised thunderhead
towers over the mountain,
shadows the pasture.

The men set down tools,
polish the stone with worn shirtsleeves.
The dark-eyed man strikes a match,
holds it to a braided ribbon of grass.
Flames lick the tawny strands,
smoke circles the stone
rising in sweet fragrance
to join the hawk in her wheeling flight.

"Kee-er? Kee-er?"
The hawk questions the men
dips a wing
then soars to tickle the underbelly
of the thunderhead.
Lightning forks;
her tail feathers flash
a fiery red
as she rides the thermals,
gliding
on the back of the wind.

The storm cloud drifts upriver.
Sunlight glistens through
a curtain of rain.
The men stand, shoulder to shoulder,
hats lifted in salute
to the hawk.

She rises into a cobalt sky
wingtips lit by a rainbow.
Her cry of greeting lingers
long after

                she is gone.

Griswold, Vermont, November 1844

Author's Note

This novel is based on a true story about my ancestors, the Pequot midwife Margery Daigo (or Dogerill) and her husband, Joseph Griswold, who lived in Vermont during the eighteenth century.

According to historical accounts, Joseph and Margery met in Connecticut, when Joseph nearly drowned in a river accident. Margery and her Pequot family, who were fishing nearby, rescued him and nursed him back to health. (Margery was already a healer, and her father was a *powwaw,* or medicine man.) As Joseph recovered, he and Margery fell in love and married, against their families' wishes. They moved to Randolph, Vermont, where Joseph farmed and Margery delivered babies and tended to sick people in the area.

At this time, marriage between whites and Native Americans was unusual but not unheard of. In its early years, Randolph had no doctor, and Margery was the only healer for miles around. Her neighbors respected the "Indian doctress" for her healing abilities and her knowledge of native herbs and plants, which could be made into medicines, or "physicks."

As time passed, Margery's father accepted his daughter's marriage. He died on one of his visits to Vermont and was buried in a field on the Griswold farm. Margery continued with her healing work until the end of her life, riding her white mare along rough roads to see her patients. Before she died, Margery's children promised to honor their grandfather by keeping his grave sacred. Margery warned that a curse would fall on anyone who disturbed the heavy stones that marked his final resting place. Years later, a farmer ignored the curse and moved the gravestones, using them to repair a stone wall. Soon bad luck plagued the farm. First, the house and barn burned. Later, another farmer lost his herd of prize cattle to tuberculosis.

I first heard of Margery Griswold from my great-uncle Carlton Griswold Ketchum, who sent me an unsigned article about her life. Griswold was a family name, and Margery came from the same Vermont town as my uncle's grandfather, so he guessed we might be related to her. I put the article in my "idea file," where it sat for twenty years.

When I finally decided to research the story, I got in touch with the Randolph, Vermont, Historical Society and received a letter from its director, Miriam (Mim) Herwig. She wrote that she had many materials related to the Griswold family, and that she was, in fact, the historian who had written the original article about Margery.

My husband and I visited Mim and her husband right away. They lived on a ridge overlooking the river valley, in a brick house built by one of Margery's nephews. The Herwigs had many documents waiting for us. When I unrolled my family tree, we matched it with Mim's information, and discovered that Margery and Joseph Griswold were my great-great-great-great-great grandparents. Mim's husband, Wes, took us across the road to the town cemetery, where Margery and Joseph Griswold were buried side by side. We could barely read the faint inscriptions, carved into the headstones long ago, yet I felt an immediate connection to my ancestors, whose legacy had lasted into the twenty-first century.

During our visit, Wes Herwig also described the so-called Indian Raid that took place in nearby Royalton during the War for Independence. In the fall of 1780, a British lieutenant brought a group of Caughnawaga Indians down from Canada to avenge the death of a British soldier. The raiders burned houses and crops in Royalton, killing some villagers and taking others captive. Randolph's militia was called up to chase after them, but the raiders fled during the night. Some of the captives experienced brutal treatment in a British prison. A few escaped and nearly starved as they struggled home. Others were released following the Peace of Paris.

As we listened to the story, I realized that my relatives had been living in Randolph at the time of the raid. I decided that this little-known slice of history would play an important role in my novel.

Daniel and Hiram's story begins in 1782, two years after the raid. The War for Independence had recently ended, establishing America as a separate country, but Vermont was still an independent republic with its own currency and a constitution that prohibited slavery. (Vermont became part of the United States in 1791.) Vermonters who fought against the British soldiers were known as Patriots or Colonials, while their rivals were called Tories. The Patriots named the British soldiers Redcoats, because of their scarlet jackets. Some Vermont Patriots joined the Continental Army, while others stayed behind to fight with their local militias. Although I don't know how my ancestors responded to these events, I have tried to stay true to the historical record as I tell their story.

A Note on Pequot History

When the first English settlers arrived in the land they called New England, the Pequots were a powerful people who controlled much of what is now eastern Connecticut. Their influence extended throughout southern New England and into Long Island. English newcomers used words such as "potent," "stately," and "rich" to describe the tribe.

Pequot people lived in villages along the coast. The women raised crops, wove baskets, and fashioned clothing from animal skins, while the men hunted and fished. Pequot tribal leaders were called sachems. Most sachems were men, but a few were women, often called squaw sachems. Although the sachem had great power, he or she ruled by consensus, which means that important decisions were made by the group or in tribal councils.

The sachem also turned to the *powwaw,* or shaman, for advice. *Powwaws* were said to possess great spiritual power, or *mundtu* (sometimes *manitou*). Birds, animals, and even inanimate objects could also exhibit *mundtu. Powwaws* acted as messengers between the physical and the spiritual world. Pequot people believed that *powwaws* could assume the form of birds, snakes, or other animals as they performed healing ceremonies and rituals. A young person became a *powwaw* through a difficult ceremony, during which he or she had to fast, stay awake for a long time, and endure pain.

The arrival of Europeans turned Pequot life upside down. Pequots took control of the fur and wampum trade, which added to their wealth, but contact with Europeans brought epidemics of smallpox and plague. The Pequots had no natural resistance to European diseases, and their healers didn't know which herbs and medicines might cure them. Sometimes entire villages disappeared.

Throughout the 1630s, skirmishes and conflicts broke out between the Pequots and the English, culminating in the Pequot massacre of 1637. In this attack, the English slaughtered hundreds of Pequot men, women, and children—burning them alive or shooting them as they tried to escape their burning fort. The English sold the Pequot survivors into slavery, splitting them among the Mohegan and Narragansett tribes.

For more than a hundred years, the Pequots continued to suffer injustice and devastating losses of population and land. Although the Pequots were granted small reserves of land in the seventeenth century, white settlers seized their hunting and fishing areas, as well as their farmland, threatening their way of life. After the War for Independence, many Pequots, along with members of southern New England and Long Island tribes, joined the Christian Brotherton Indians and moved to Oneida Indian land in New York State.

By the 1950s, the Pequots' situation was desperate. Tribal members had scattered and only two Pequot half-sisters lived on a piece of Pequot land in eastern Connecticut. They held on to this small holding until their deaths. In 1983, after years of legal battles, the Mashantucket branch of the Pequots finally gained tribal recognition; Eastern Pequots received preliminary recognition in 2004. Mashantucket Pequots moved back onto their land and built the highly successful Foxwoods casino in Mashantucket, Connecticut.

In spite of all that the Pequots suffered, their culture has shown strength and resilience. Tribal leaders have announced plans to revitalize the language, and the Mashantuckets have revived the ancient tradition known as Schemitzun, or the Feast of First Corn and Dance. The festival brings thousands of Native American dancers, drummers, and singers to Pequot land to celebrate the ripening of the first, or "green," corn in an enormous powwow. Deep drumbeats, jingling bells, and powerful voices resound as the grand procession of dancers moves into the huge arena. Circling in their beaded shawls, feathered headdresses, fringed deerskin, and flowing skirts, the dancers flow under the canvas roof.

Down the hill from the Schemitzun arena is the Mashantucket Pequot Museum and Research Center, a monument to Pequot culture and history. The great hall, with its soaring wall of glass, resembles a giant wigwam, large enough to contain the spirit and courage of the Pequots who lost their lives over the years—and of those who carry the dreams of their people into the future.

About the Pequot Language

The Treaty of Hartford, signed in 1638, made it illegal for Pequots to speak their own language, but this rule had little effect. Changes in the language occurred as missionaries began to convert Pequots to Christianity in the eighteenth century. Because the Pequot and Mohegan languages are so closely related, linguists refer to the language as Mohegan-Pequot, and the small vocabulary that has been collected and passed down over the years is probably derived from the marriage of these two languages. Research on the remnants of Pequot language is ongoing. I used the following sources: James Noyes's "Vocabulary of Pequot," dated 1669–79 and Ezra Stiles's "Wordlist of Mohegan-Pequot," dated 1793 (both manuscripts are in the Beinecke Library, Yale University). I also relied on the informative displays at the Mashantucket Pequot Museum and Research Center. The works of Frank Speck, an early-twentieth-century anthropologist, were helpful, as was *The Pequots in Southern New England: The Rise and Fall of an American Indian Nation*, edited by Laurence M. Hauptman and James D. Wherry (Norman: University of Oklahoma Press, 1990). Melissa Jayne Fawcett's book *Medicine Trail: The Life and Lessons of Gladys Tantaquidgeon* (Tucson: University of Arizona Press, 2000) provides essential background on Mohegan history, language, and cultural life.